#7

FLIRTING

DIANE HOH

SCHOLASTIC INC.
New York Toronto London Auckland Sydney

ISBN 0-590-33687-8

Copyright © 1985 by Diane Hoh. All rights reserved. Published by Scholastic Inc.

12 11 10 9 8 7 6 5 4 3 2 1   7   5 6 7 8 9/8 0/9

CHEERLEADERS

FLIRTING

CHEERLEADERS

CHAPTER

Mary Ellen Kirkwood walked slowly from one display to the next, gently fingering delicate gold chains, silken print scarves, and her favorites, gold and silver earrings in all shapes and sizes. She sighed with yearning.

A tall, elegant woman in a chic black dress came over to Mary Ellen and said hello. Her hair, its honey-blonde color almost identical to Mary Ellen's, was pulled back from her finely chiseled features into a smooth bun.

"I've seen you in here before," the woman said, smiling. "Aren't you one of the Tarenton cheerleaders?"

Mary Ellen nodded, pleased. "I'm Mary Ellen Kirkwood."

"I'm Else Gunderson. I own this shop." She looked at Mary Ellen carefully, taking in her blonde hair, blue eyes, and perfect figure.

Because they were the only two people in the store, they began to talk. Mary Ellen, not usually so friendly, was flattered by the woman's attention and found herself confiding to the woman about her plans to become a New York model when she finished high school.

"Well, you certainly have the face and figure for it," Mrs. Gunderson said. "I just hope you have the money."

Money? Mary Ellen had exactly eighty-seven dollars. It was all she had left out of what she'd earned doing laundry for her neighbors for a while. She'd had to quit. It just wasn't possible to be a full-time Varsity cheerleader and hold down a part-time job. None of the Tarenton cheerleaders worked.

But then, Mary Ellen thought with a certain amount of resentment, none of the others *needed* to.

"You'll need money to get to New York," Mrs. Gunderson explained matter-of-factly. Ticking off items on her ringed fingers, she added, "First and last month's rent in an incredibly expensive city, security deposit, utilities, cab and subway fare, the cost of installing a telephone, food, clothing. And you'll need anywhere from five hundred to a thousand dollars for a really good photographer to do your portfolio. That's a collection of still and action shots. Every major modeling agency requires them."

"You know a lot about it," Mary Ellen said with respect.

The woman smiled. "I should. I was a model in Chicago for five-and-a-half years." Still smiling, she glanced around the store and said, "But I like it better here.

"Well," she added, "I suppose it'll be easier for you. If you had money problems, you wouldn't be in here, would you? You young girls all seem to have money these days. Thank goodness. I don't know where my business would be without you."

The expression on Mary Ellen's face must have been revealing, because after a moment or two Mrs. Gunderson said softly, "Oh. I see.

"Well, then," she said briskly, ignoring Mary Ellen's embarrassment, "how would you like to earn some money and gain a little modeling experience at the same time? I've been thinking of hiring someone like yourself to model some clothes out in the mall."

"Model?" Mary Ellen parroted.

"Yes. All the stores here have a little enclosed platform out in front for just that purpose. I've never used mine, but maybe it's time."

A chance to actually model? Some of Marnie's gorgeous things? Mary Ellen couldn't believe it. Life had seemed so dreary earlier that day. Nothing *good* was happening. And now here it was, falling right into her lap!

"It's hard work," Mrs. Gunderson warned. "It can be very boring and very tiring."

Boring? Tiring? Mary Ellen just grinned. She couldn't wait to shout, "Are you kidding? Yes, yes, I'll take it! When do I start?"

But before she could get the words out, Mrs. Gunderson added, "I'll pay you a small salary, of course, and give you a discount on everything in the store." And then she said, "I'll need you Saturdays and three afternoons a week. The afternoons are a must. That's when business has been the slowest. I need someone or something out there to bring in the customers, and you'd be it."

Mary Ellen's heart sank like a stone. Saturdays. Three afternoons a week. Not two, which she could handle easily enough, but three. Mrs. Gunderson had been very definite about that.

But Ardith Engborg, Tarenton's cheerleading coach, was equally definite about practice three times a week. And forget Saturdays — there was just no way she could work on Saturday. There were games and practices and pep rallies. Mary Ellen was sure the only acceptable excuse for missing any of them was death, which she suspected was also the *punishment* for missing one of them.

Sensing a dilemma, Mrs. Gunderson smiled and said, "You don't have to give me an answer right now, Mary Ellen. But I would appreciate hearing from you by the end of the week, okay?"

A customer came in and Mrs. Gunderson turned to take care of her. Before she left, she said, "I really think this is a good idea. So if you can't do it, I'll probably look for someone else. Maybe you could recommend someone?"

Mary Ellen thanked her for the offer, promised to let her know soon, and left, her head whirling. A salary. A discount on all those gorgeous clothes. There probably isn't a single, solitary thing in that store that I wouldn't be happy wearing, she thought, smiling.

The sight of Vanessa Barlow coming her way wiped the smile off her face. Dressed in a terrific

4

black leather outfit and bright red boots, she was headed straight for Marnie's.

She probably hasn't bought anything new in the last fifteen minutes, Mary Ellen thought nastily, and is starting to suffer withdrawal pains.

Mary Ellen had tried not to speak to Vanessa Barlow since that horrible time when "Vicious Van" had planted some terrible rumors about Mary Ellen shoplifting, right there at Marnie's. One day, Mary Ellen thought grimly as she walked past Vanessa without a word, I'm going to get even with her. She really needs to be paid back.

Vanessa had also planted some nasty rumors about another cheerleader, Angie Poletti, spreading it around school that Angie's unexpected appearance on the honor roll was due to cheating.

A horrible thought struck Mary Ellen: If *I* don't take that job, Vanessa will get it. I just know she will. Mrs. Gunderson would have to be blind not to notice that Vanessa would make a terrific model.

Determined to talk Mrs. Engborg into letting her miss just one tiny little practice each week, and equally determined to talk Mrs. Gunderson into forgetting about the Saturday part of it (after all, she *had* said the weekday afternoons were the most important), Mary Ellen hurried to the mall bus stop.

But the next day at practice, Mrs. Engborg said *no*. "If I give in to you," she said firmly, "I'll have to give in to the others when they ask. You're the squad captain, Mary Ellen. You're supposed to set an example." As she turned away, she said, "Everyone gives up things for extracurricular activities, Mary Ellen. You're not the only one."

Mary Ellen stared at her coach's retreating back and thought bitterly, Oh, yeah? What has Nancy Goldstein given up? A couple of shopping trips? She can make those up on Saturday mornings. And Pres? He still has his beloved Porsche, doesn't he? Olivia Evans has Walt and Walt has Olivia, and Nancy's got Josh. So what is everybody else giving up, I'd like to know?

Angry and frustrated, Mary Ellen's timing was off during the entire practice session.

"Mary Ellen! Stop pouting and concentrate!" Mrs. Engborg ordered sharply, after the squad captain miscalculated a Toe Touch and made a poor landing, twisting her ankle slightly.

Mary Ellen made a face, more from annoyance than pain. She was sick and tired of being yelled at. She was sick of Olivia and Walt cooing at each other and wildly applauding each other's gymnastic feats. She was sick of Angie's constant cheerfulness, Nancy's cool efficiency, and Pres's arrogance.

Why had she wanted to be a cheerleader in the first place? To be Somebody Special. Well, she was somebody special — at least in Tarenton — but she was still poor. And she needed that job. If it weren't for cheerleading, she'd snap up that offer so fast, the lighted sign out in front of Marnie's would short-circuit.

But I *am* a cheerleader, she told herself finally, and I'm the squad captain. It's what I wanted.

And now that I've got it, I'm stuck with it, so I'd better shape up.

And she concentrated on concentrating. But she didn't improve much during the last half hour of practice.

Avoiding a lecture from Ardith Engborg by hurrying immediately to the locker room, she raced through her shower and dried her hair before confronting Angie Poletti at the long mirror over the sinks.

"Angie," she began, pulling on a pair of gray corduroy slacks, "when are we going to get back at Vanessa? You know we never really have."

Angie stopped brushing her hair and stared at Mary Ellen, her eyes were wide. Angie was the perfect cheerleader: wholesome, eager, loving every minute of it.

"Are you serious? *I'm* not messing with Vanessa. That girl is dangerous! Anyway, it's all water under the bridge."

"Let it go, Mary Ellen," Nancy said quietly as she passed them on her way out. "It's way over and done with."

Mary Ellen noticed as Nancy passed that, as usual, every dark, silky strand of hair was in place, every bit of eye makeup blended perfectly, and a blue plaid skirt and blue sweater were perfectly coordinated on that perfect body.

How do you *do* it, Nancy? she wondered silently. You just worked out for two solid hours and you look as if you just stepped out of a beauty parlor instead of a gym.

Aloud, she said sarcastically, "I could have sworn I was talking to *Angie!*"

Nancy shrugged and left.

"Angie, c'mon!" Mary Ellen persisted. "Van needs to be taught a lesson or she'll just go on doing rotten things. If we put our heads together, we can come up with something terrific. I know we can."

Angie shook her head. "Nancy's right," she said, buttoning the collar of her green knit shirt. "Everybody's forgotten about it now, anyway. So should we."

Just as Mary Ellen was wondering resentfully if the time would ever come when Nancy Goldstein would be *wrong* about something, Olivia Evans emerged from her shower. Her small, slender figure wrapped in a maroon towel, she bent forward at the waist to brush her light brown hair away from her scalp. Still in that position, she called, "You guys going to Walt's party?"

"Party? What party?" the girls asked in one voice.

Olivia straightened up, facing them. Cheeks flushed from bending over, she was the picture of health, in spite of her tiny frame. No one who knew Olivia now could believe that she had been seriously ill as a child, had spent much of her childhood as an invalid. She didn't look or act like one now.

"Walt's giving a party after the Garrison game Friday night." She laughed. "A victory party, we hope!"

Mary Ellen frowned. "Nobody said anything to me."

Angie and Olivia exchanged looks, meaning,

Why is Mary Ellen so paranoid? "Read my lips," Olivia said. "I am at this very moment asking you to come to Walt's party. You know him — too busy flying off in ten directions at the same time to bother with the details of his own party. He left the inviting to me." She sighed. "And the shopping and the decorating and . . . oh, well, I guess it's nice to be needed."

"I wouldn't know," Angie said sadly, and the other two laughed. Angie was between boy-friends, and not very happy about it. But since Angie was never very unhappy for too long, nobody worried about her.

"Maybe you'll meet somebody positively gorgeous and fascinating at the party," Olivia said as she slipped into jeans and a sweatshirt. "I think some of Walt's parents' friends are going to be there, too."

"Television people?" Angie asked, her eyes wide.

She's almost beautiful when she's excited, Mary Ellen thought with some surprise. Funny, I always think of Angie as the plain one on the squad. But she really isn't.

"I guess so," Olivia answered Angie. "They're all at Walt's house all the time, anyway, because his parents' talk show is taped right there in the house. Walt's used to the camera crew being around. They don't even impress him anymore."

"Well, they impress *me*!" Angie said. "And you're right, maybe I *will* meet somebody fan-tastic. Maybe a producer or a director. Anyway, I love parties. Tell Walt I'll be there."

"Me, too," Mary Ellen added.

She thought later, as she walked into the little bedroom she shared with her younger sister Gemma and threw her books on the bed, one good thing about going to a party after a game is you don't have to worry about digging up something great to wear. It was perfectly okay to wear your uniform to an after-game party. And she loved her uniform. How could anyone not love the thick white sweater with the big red "T" on the front, and the short, full red skirt with the white pleats that flared out around her when she jumped? It made her Somebody at Tarenton High, and in Tarenton itself.

But if I don't start earning some money pretty quick, she thought grimly, staring out the window, I'm never going to have the chance to be Somebody any place *but* Tarenton. If only there were some way I could accept Mrs. Gunderson's offer.

CHAPTER

Angie wished her brother Andrew would snap out of it. Watching him pick at his food at the dinner table night after night was just too depressing.

"He's not eating enough to keep a bird alive," her mother said softly as she and Angie loaded the dishwasher after Andrew had gone to his room and closed the door. The kitchen smelled of permanent-wave solution, as it always did — one of the disadvantages of living upstairs when your mother's beauty parlor is *downstairs.* Angie never complained about the smell because her mother, a widow for many years, worked hard to support Angie and her brothers.

"It's Kerry," Angie said. "He hasn't gotten over her."

"Such a lovely girl," Mrs. Poletti commented, sighing as she scoured a pan in the sink. "I didn't see her as the sort who would drop our Andrew for someone as flashy as Preston Tilford. I thought she had more sense than that. She isn't the kind who would be impressed by his money."

"Well, Pres sort of has a way of convincing girls that they can't live without him," her daughter said grimly. Pres was important to the cheerleading squad and Angie considered him her friend, as well. But he could have had practically any girl in school. He could have left Kerry alone. He *knew* she was Andrew's girl.

Pres really seemed to care about Kerry, Angie had to admit that. But it hurt her to see her younger brother so miserable.

"He needs to meet somebody new," her mother said softly. "That's the surest way to heal a broken heart. Don't you know some nice girl, honey? Someone Andrew would like?"

Angie laughed. "Ma, *I* need advice to the lovelorn as much as Andrew does. When's the last time I had a date?"

Her mother gave her a hug and said, "Well, never mind anybody else. *I'm* crazy about both of you."

Then Angie remembered Walt's party and told her mother about it. "Maybe I'll meet someone really terrific, Ma. And if I do," she added, laughing, "I'll promise I'll see if he has a younger sister for Andrew."

At school the next day, there were Pres and Kerry, walking through the halls, holding hands as if nobody else existed in this world. Angie thought they looked so incongruous together: Pres's sleek, dark blond head and wide shoulders next to chubby, dark-haired Kerry; Pres's sophistication next to Kerry's innocence. But she had to admit, too, that Pres had changed since he'd met Kerry. He wasn't always eyeing girls these days, and he seemed a little friendlier. Not quite so self-centered and aloof. Kerry had shattered the hopes of a lot of girls at Tarenton High when she snagged Pres.

"Not mine," Nancy said at lunch when Angie repeated the thought out loud. "He always liked himself a lot more than *I* liked him."

"Sure, you say that now," Shelley Eismar said as she and her twin Cathleen put their trays on the table, "now that you've got Josh!"

Nancy laughed. "You guys going to Walt's party?"

"Sure," Cathleen answered, sitting down and taking a bite of her sandwich. "I hear Vanessa's going, too. And she's bringing a new boyfriend. Some football player from college. Older type. Another Einstein, I'm sure."

Nancy said, "The only boy she ever dated with brains was Pres."

Cathleen nodded. "Brawn over brains, that's Vanessa's speed."

"Well, it works out well," Shelley said, grinning, "because anyone with the brain of a pea couldn't take Vanessa for more than two-and-a-half minutes."

They spent the rest of their lunch period talking about the upcoming game with Garrison.

Tarenton won. But not by much. The final score was 76-74 and by the time it was over, everyone in the crowded gym was hoarse. It had been a tough fight, and the Tarenton Varsity

Basketball team had performed well.

Ardith Engborg wished she could say the same for her Varsity Cheerleaders.

"Mary Ellen, honestly!" she said in exasperation as they all prepared to leave the gym. "Where was your head tonight? You've done that Pony Mount Sit with Pres hundreds of times. I can't believe you lost your balance!"

Neither could Mary Ellen. Stumbling off Pres's back and landing on her bottom on the gym floor had been one of the most humiliating moments of her entire life. Her timing had been off all night, and that had just been the worst in a series of bad moves on her part. She'd had a terrible time concentrating on the game, which had had some really hairy moments. She'd passed off most of the important name cheers to Nancy, and then she'd goofed with Pres. He had been really disgusted with her, she could tell. And she'd asked for it.

She knew why, though, and no one else did. That afternoon, she had finally given up on getting enough time off from practice to accept Mrs. Gunderson's offer, so she had called Marnie's owner and turned down the job. She wasn't at all happy about it. And it showed.

No one said a word to her in the locker room. They were all laughing and jumping up and down and hugging each other, but she could tell she wasn't being included. It hurt, but she knew she had it coming. When one person was off as much as she'd been, it made the whole squad look bad.

The first person she ran into at Walt's party was Vanessa Barlow.

Oh, no, Mary Ellen groaned silently. I haven't even had anything to *eat* yet!

"Hi, Mary Ellen," Vanessa purred. She was wearing her usual on her arm: a tall, tanned, very good-looking athletic type, wearing a ski sweater and corduroys. His shoulders were as wide as the Grand Canyon, but Mary Ellen knew his mind was probably about as deep as a dry creek bed. And having a tan in Tarenton at this time of year meant a sun lamp. He was as vain as Vanessa, if that was possible.

She brushed by the couple without speaking.

"Oh, Mary Ellen," Vanessa sing-songed after her, "guess what? Guess where I'm working now?"

No, Mary Ellen thought. No, she's *not*. Not already. She can't be.

But she was. Vanessa had taken the modeling job at Marnie's. Mrs. Gunderson, she told Mary Ellen's back, had called her that very afternoon just before she left for the game, and practically begged her to model for Marnie's. "Of course I said yes!" she said gleefully. "Why on earth would anyone turn down such a fabulous offer?"

She knows, Mary Ellen realized. She knows perfectly well I had a crack at it first and she's rubbing it in. That thought was followed by a very strong, very clear desire to turn around and strangle Vanessa — very, very slowly and very, very thoroughly.

Instead, Mary Ellen walked away without a word. But she was more determined than ever not to let the evening go by without doing something nasty to Vanessa Barlow. Her being the superintendent of schools' daughter didn't frighten Mary Ellen.

Olivia Evans loved Walt Manners' home. Although she'd been there many times since they'd started dating, she still felt really good as soon as she walked through the front door of the darling log-and-glass house his parents had built deep in the woods. The atmosphere inside was so casual and cozy, nothing like the modern, efficiently run household Olivia was used to.

But then, she reminded herself, Mr. and Mrs. Manners were "show biz."

Walt hung her coat in the hall closet and led her into the family room, already full of people, some sitting, some milling around by the food table. Rock music blasted away and the smell of pine filled the air, which Olivia knew meant a pine-cone fire blazing away in the big stone fireplace that nearly filled one wall. She saw Mary Ellen sitting alone on the couch, Nancy and Josh cutting across the room to join Angie at the French doors overlooking the woods, and Vanessa flirting with a gorgeous hunk in a ski sweater. Pres and Kerry were standing by the food, but they weren't eating anything. They were just staring at each other.

I'm glad Walt and I don't act that dippy in public, Olivia thought. It's just too embarrassing. But she wouldn't mind if Walt paid a little more attention to her tonight than he usually did at parties. The Life of the Party, that was her Walt.

Always clowning, always joking, except when he was cheerleading — then his strong, stocky body did amazing routines. It made it hard on the girl he was with. Sometimes Olivia felt like a piece of wallpaper on the wall, a feeling she wasn't really wild about.

She went over and sat down on the couch beside Mary Ellen while Walt went to get something to eat.

And didn't come back.

She knew perfectly well what he was doing: He'd found an audience somewhere and was entertaining them. It didn't help her any to understand that, since Walt had never been a part of his parents' television show, clowning in public was his way of getting the attention they'd always had and he'd never shared.

"But it drives me crazy," she told Mary Ellen. "I might just as well come alone to these things."

Mary Ellen shrugged. She wasn't feeling very sympathetic. Still stinging from Vanessa's ability to take the job she had wanted so badly for herself, she certainly didn't feel like listening to Olivia's whining. Without a word, she got up and left.

Before Olivia had a chance to feel offended, someone took Mary Ellen's place on the couch. A young man Olivia had never seen before said, "Hi, gorgeous. How come you're sitting here all by your lonesome? I thought cheerleaders always had hordes of football captains chasing after them twenty-four hours a day."

It was almost as if Olivia had asked for the exact opposite of Walt to suddenly appear at her side. This person was as tall and thin as Walt was stocky and round-faced. She had never seen Walt any way but well-scrubbed and clean-shaven, while the person beside her had a day's growth of beard, and his plaid shirt and khaki pants needed to be tossed into a washing machine. Still . . . he looked interesting. And Walt shouldn't have deserted her.

"You're not from Tarenton High," she said. He was too old. He had to be at least twenty-one, maybe older. It was hard to tell with that yucky razor stubble.

"You kidding? No, I'm one of your working-class types, the sort without which the world wouldn't go around. Actually, I'm the boom man on the media event, which takes place in this very house every morning. They call me Boomer. Without yours truly, you'd still be able to see the picture, but you wouldn't be able to hear word one of the fascinating exchange of ideas between my employers and their guests."

"That sounds interesting," Olivia said politely.

"It's a living," he said, shrugging his thin shoulders. "Hardly what I had in mind when I studied communications, but it buys food. And drink. Especially drink. Speaking of which, can I get you something?"

Olivia looked around the room. She saw Pres and Kerry trying to dance in the crowded room, and Nancy and Josh sitting at a small table playing Trivial Pursuit. Angie was leaning against the wall talking to a tall, red-haired boy Olivia didn't know, and Evie Caird was talking to Mary Ellen at the food table.

But Walt Manners was nowhere in sight.

Olivia had never had a drink before. Her mother's endless lectures on good health stuck in her mind. But she was a little flattered that Boomer thought she was old enough. Besides, she was sick of sitting around with nothing to do while Walt went off by himself and had a good time.

"Sure," she said heartily. "I'll have whatever you're having."

He raised an eyebrow, but got up without a word and came back a few minutes later with a paper cup in each hand.

"You *have* had this stuff before, right?" he asked as he sat back down. "I mean, I don't want to be accused of corrupting anyone."

"Oh, sure," Olivia fibbed, taking a sip of what looked like plain old lemonade.

It was *not* plain old lemonade. Boomer grinned as she coughed when the liquid hit her tongue and her throat, causing a burning sensation that lasted a few seconds. Then the warmth spread inside her and she began to feel . . . well, not so bad. Not so bad. She took another sip and then another. Before long, she began to feel very warm and relaxed.

So relaxed that when Boomer slipped an arm around her shoulders, she didn't push it away.

She hadn't realized how thirsty she was. When the cup was empty, Boomer got a refill for her, and she finished that quickly.

"It's awfully hot in here," she complained. "Must be because it's so crowded." And the music suddenly seemed awfully loud to her. From somewhere far away she heard Walt's deep laugh.

Still entertaining everybody, she thought angrily. Everybody but *me*.

Thank goodness Boomer had come along. He was kind and attentive, the way a boy should be. And so good-looking. Just adorable. Funny she hadn't noticed that right away.

"C'mon!" he said suddenly, taking her hand and pulling her to her feet. "Let's go someplace quiet and . . . talk."

"Where we goin'?" The room played hide-and-seek as Olivia stood up. The few drops left in her cup dripped onto her cheerleading skirt.

"Oh, darn!" she cried, staring down at the small wet spot on the red wool. "Now I'll have to take it to the cly dreaners."

Realizing what she had said, she lifted her head and giggled, then clapped one hand over her mouth to hide the giggling. He'd think she was a stupid, silly child.

He grinned. "C'mon," he said. "Let's get away from this crowd."

"O-kay! But maybe I'd better hang on to you. This floor is really shaky. Must be from all those people dancing."

"Yeah, must be. Here, hold on to big old Boomer. I'll take good care of the little lady."

Ten minutes later, Vanessa Barlow came out of the bathroom and stumbled onto a sight that made her heart beat fast with joy. Olivia Evans, Walt Manners' girl friend, was in a bedroom, necking like crazy with some scruffy-looking skinny guy.

I think I just died and went to heaven, Vanessa rejoiced. Olivia took the spot on Varsity Cheerleading that I should have had, and I've never had the chance to get even. And here is that chance, right in front of me!

Smiling happily, she hurried off to find Walt. I'm going to snag two for the price of one, she thought giddily, scanning the crowd in front of her for Walt's round, good-natured face. I'll wipe that smile off his face so fast his eyes will spin.

And then there he was, right in front of her.

CHAPTER

When Mary Ellen found Vanessa's date standing by himself in a corner, she walked over quickly and stuck out her hand.

"Hi! I'm Mary Ellen Kirkwood, a friend of Van's. You must be Dick Rigby." She hadn't had any trouble finding out his name.

"Oh, hi. Yeah, that's me. You a cheerleader?" he asked, glancing at the big red "T" on Mary Ellen's sweater.

Oh, brother. Terrific, Mary Ellen thought happily, a typical Vanessa date. No extra room in his sweater, but plenty in his head. Perfect.

"It was nice of you to bring Van," she said softly. "After all she's been through, it's good for her to get out among normal people."

He frowned. "She been sick?"

Mary Ellen shrugged. "Well, no, not really. How long have you known Van?"

"I just met her."

Good. "Well, she hasn't been exactly sick,"

Mary Ellen continued. "It was more . . . well, you know." She tapped a finger lightly against her temple.

He frowned and looked blank.

She sighed. This wasn't going to be easy. She had a real Neanderthal on her hands here. Probably terrific in the backseat of a car, though.

"Well, she seems okay now," she said. "I mean, she hasn't done anything real strange tonight, has she?" She waited a moment and then added carefully, "Yet?"

A faint light appeared in his big, beautiful blue eyes.

Well, about time. She closed in for the kill. "I mean, I never actually *saw* anything myself. It was probably all just silly gossip. I just can't imagine Vanessa actually throwing food at people in a public restaurant, can you? Or taking all of the coats at a party and tossing them in the swimming pool? And the thought of her running out on the court at one of the basketball games and pretending she was a cheerleader, well, that's just too silly."

He was hanging on every word.

"Of course," she added thoughtfully, "she *did* always want to be a cheerleader, so maybe. . . . No, it *couldn't* have happened. I mean, I was at every one of those games and I never saw anything like that happen."

He glanced around the room nervously. "Gee, she *seems* fine," he said shakily.

"Well, sure she does," Mary Ellen said enthusiastically, giving him a little punch on the arm. "Gosh, I wouldn't want you to worry or

23

anything. Like I said, I'm sure it was just stupid gossip. You know how some people like to talk!"

As she turned to leave, she added casually, "Of course, it is true that you can't always tell about people, don't you think? I mean, they may seem a certain way and then something happens to set them off and, well . . . it must be so embarrassing for the people they're with!" She shuddered, flashing him a brilliant smile and called, "Have a good time tonight!" and walked away.

She stopped at the food table and turned, just in time to see him grab his jacket and head for the front door, not even looking over his shoulder as he went.

I do *not* feel like a rotten person, she thought, smiling. Vanessa had it coming. Besides, she wouldn't have any trouble finding a replacement. Later, when she saw Vanessa looking around the room with a puzzled frown, she felt only a tiny twinge of conscience.

If she'd known what Vanessa had just done to Olivia and Walt, she wouldn't even have felt that tiny trace.

It had been easy enough for Vanessa to locate Walt. All she'd had to do was look for the nearest laughing crowd, and there he was, right smack in the middle. He was doing impersonations. She was delighted to see the crowd. The more people who knew what sweet, quiet little Olivia was doing, the better.

"Oh, Walt," she called, waving a hand in the air to get his attention. "Walt, could I see you for just a sec?"

A few people looked her way, but not Walt. She wasn't going to be able to get his attention from the fringes of the crowd, that was for sure.

She elbowed her way closer, and called his name again. This time he heard her and, frowning at being interrupted, asked her what she wanted. Happily for her, he stayed right where he was, which meant she had to call out in order for him to hear her.

"I think there's something you should see," she told him. "It's Olivia. . . ."

That got him. "What's wrong?" he asked, obviously alarmed. His audience, sensing some excitement, turned their attention to Vanessa, which was exactly what she wanted.

"Oh, nothing, really," Vanessa answered in a tone that clearly indicated just the opposite was true. "I just think you might be interested in what your girl friend is up to."

"Where is she?"

"Follow me."

He did. And so did everyone else. Vanessa thought with amusement, as they made their way back to the bedroom, that they must look like a parade. Right. And Walt was the clown. He was going to feel foolish when they all saw what Vanessa had seen! She hoped fervently that Olivia hadn't come to her senses and dumped the guy and ruined everything.

She hadn't. It looked to Vanessa as if neither one of them had moved since she'd first seen them. They were still totally engrossed in what they were doing, which was necking as if they'd been going together for ages. Olivia's arms were around Boomer's neck and he held her close.

"Olivia!" Walt shouted furiously. "What do you think you're doing?"

Vanessa giggled, as did several others in the crowd. What did it *look* like she was doing?

The guy holding Olivia in a death grip jumped a foot when Walt yelled. He released Olivia, who looked around in a daze.

Why, she's been drinking, Vanessa thought with surprise. I didn't know little Olivia drank. She doesn't even know what she's doing. But I'll bet that won't cut any ice with her boyfriend.

It didn't. Walt didn't even seem to notice what a fog Olivia was in. His round face flushed with anger and he reached down and grabbed Olivia's wrist.

"Get up!" he demanded.

She stood up shakily and stared at him. "Walt?"

"Take it easy, man," Boomer said. "She's had a few too many."

"Yeah? Well, I can guess where she got it!" Walt retorted angrily. "Don't you have anything better to do with your time than to get high school girls drunk?"

Then he turned back to Olivia, who looked very confused. "C'mon," he said coldly. "We're getting out of here." He pulled on her arm, yanking her along behind him as he made his way through the crowd and down the hall, grabbing their jackets out of the closet as he went. Olivia stumbled once, but he never even slowed down.

When they had disappeared, slamming the front door after them, Vanessa turned to the crowd and said, "Well, I must say, our cheerleaders certainly set a fine example for the rest of us!" and noticed with satisfaction that quite a few people in the crowd nodded in agreement.

She hadn't been looking forward to this party. She hated being at parties where all of the Varsity Cheerleaders sat around in their sweet little uniforms, laughing and talking together as if they were a private club. It just made her remember again the humiliation of not being picked for the squad.

But this party hadn't been like the others. *This* one had been fun!

If Mrs. Engborg heard about Olivia's behavior (and Vanessa was just sure that she would), maybe she'd kick her right off the squad. And would need an immediate replacement.

Vanessa smiled and left the crowd, anxious to reclaim her date for the evening.

Walt practically pushed Olivia into the Jeep, tossing her jacket in after her. When he got in on the driver's side, he turned the ignition key with an angry twist and the Jeep roared out of the driveway toward the main road. Olivia sat quietly, hands folded in her lap.

"I don't believe this!" he shouted, his usually mild manner completely gone. "I leave you alone for five minutes. . . ."

"You left me alone a lot longer than five minutes," Olivia interrupted, "and you do it to me all the time. I'm *sick* of it."

He stared at her for a minute, before returning his eyes to the road ahead. "What are you talking about?"

"You do this to me all the time," she said, crying. "Every party we go to, the minute you walk in the front door, you're looking for an audience. I might as well go by myself." The fresh air and Walt's anger had cleared her head, and she had decided they might as well get things out in the open right now.

He was silent for a few minutes. She'd never complained before, and he didn't know how to take it. Did he really do that, ignore her the way she said? Well, even if he did, that wasn't any excuse for what *she'd* done. He still couldn't believe it.

"You acted like a . . . a tramp, right in front of the whole school!" he yelled. "You made me look like a fool. Everyone knows you're supposed to be my girl, and there you were, making out like a bandit with that jerk!"

"All you care about is how you look," Olivia shouted, staring straight ahead. "I don't think you *feel* bad at all, or that you're worried about me not being your girl anymore. You're just *mad*. Because it made you look bad."

"Don't *you* care how it looked?" he snapped, wheeling the Jeep around a sharp curve.

"Yes. I care. It was a stupid thing to do, and I wouldn't have done it if I hadn't had those drinks. That was a stupid thing to do, too. And I'm sorry."

"Right."

"I *am* sorry. But I was just so tired of being

alone. I was supposed to be with you, but you weren't around. You left me alone the minute we got there."

"So you picked up some bum and fell all over him. Smart, Olivia, real smart."

"I *said* it was stupid. But at least I said I was sorry. I haven't heard you say you were sorry for leaving me alone that whole time."

He didn't say it. He didn't say anything. He just drove silently on into town, but every time he shifted she could feel his anger in the way he grabbed the stick shift.

She couldn't believe he was willing to leave things like this. Walt was important to her. She wasn't that close to anyone else. She'd been picked as a Varsity Cheerleader because of her ability, not because she was popular. She wasn't. It was all those years of exercise, trying to prove once and for all that she was physically fit, that had won her a place on the squad, not the fact that everybody knew her and liked her. Getting to know people took her a long time. And Walt hadn't been an exception.

But once they had gotten to know each other, it had been wonderful. They'd taken long, quiet walks, talked on the phone constantly, and they'd studied together, because if they hadn't, Walt wouldn't have finished half his assignments. And they'd held each other tightly when things got to be too much: parents, school, whatever.

The only real problem they'd had was Walt's need to be on stage all the time. But she'd never intended to let that pull them apart.

She tried once more as they came to a screeching halt in front of her house. "Walt. . . ."

"Forget it," he said rudely. He reached across in front of her to push her door open. He wasn't even going to get out and walk her to the door.

She looked over at him with tears in her eyes. "I didn't know what I was doing," she said softly.

He looked away.

Without another word, she got out and walked unsteadily up the path to her front door. The Jeep roared away.

But the worst wasn't over yet, she realized as she noticed the light in the living room window. As always, her mother was waiting up.

And she'll know, Olivia thought miserably. She'll know I've been drinking. She leaned against the door, tears sliding down her cheeks, wishing she had never been born.

CHAPTER

At the party, Mary Ellen was just biting into a potato chip when Patrick Henley appeared in the doorway. Her stomach turned over, as it always did when Patrick came into her life. Sometimes she wished she saw more of Patrick, but then when she did see him, the feelings he aroused in her made her wish she hadn't seen him at all. Almost.

Patrick Henley was everything Mary Ellen wanted in a boy — except rich. Patrick not only wasn't rich, he had his own garbage truck in Tarenton, and what's more, he enjoyed having it.

"Where would Tarenton be without us?" he had asked Mary Ellen more than once. "Where would the *world* be without us?"

Mary Ellen had no trouble admitting that garbage certainly had to be picked up and disposed of somehow. She just didn't want tall, gorgeous, funny, sweet, exciting Patrick Henley to do the disposing.

Everybody liked Patrick. Every girl in school who wasn't already in love tripped over her own feet trying to get to Patrick Henley.

But there was only one girl for Patrick and that girl was Mary Ellen Kirkwood, the blonde and beautiful captain of the Tarenton Varsity Cheerleaders.

And, Patrick thought ruefully as he stood in the doorway watching her, she wants no part of me until I'm behind the wheel of a Porsche. Like Pres. He had hoped, a little, when he started seeing Pres and Kerry everywhere together, that Mary Ellen would turn to him. But every time he ran into her, she had her guard up. Once in a while, he would practically take her in this arms and she would yield, sweetly, willingly. He had always been able to read in those big, beautiful blue eyes that she shared his feelings. But Mary Ellen was a girl who knew what she wanted — and what she wanted did *not* include a garbage collector boyfriend.

Still, it wouldn't kill her to dance with him.

Mary Ellen saw him coming and her breath caught in her throat. He was wearing crisp chinos and a blue V-necked sweater over a tan button-down shirt. He looked about as much like a garbage collector as Pres looked like Santa Claus.

But, she reminded herself as Patrick, without a word, took her into his arms and began moving slowly through the crowd, he *owns* his own garbage truck! And what's worse, he intends to own more!

That worked for about three seconds, keeping

her stiff and unyielding against Patrick's warm, solid chest. But the music was soft and dreamy, Patrick felt wonderful, and when she looked up, he was smiling down at her. Her bones melted. She sagged against him, thinking, Oh, Patrick.

When he was holding her in his arms, she had to fight so hard to remember the things she needed to remember: that she was sick of being poor. That someday she *had* to be able to walk into a store like Marnie's with a wallet full of charge cards and leave it with her arms full of packages. Patrick couldn't do that for her.

But he certainly could do other things for her. Like making her feel safe and loved and, valuable, and *so* sexy. Patrick made her feel important in a way that had nothing to do with the fact that she was captain of the Tarenton Cheerleaders.

"Let's get out of here," he said in a husky voice, his mouth against her hair.

She shouldn't. She knew she shouldn't. Don't do this, Mary Ellen, the little inner voice that monitored her every move, warned.

"Okay," she whispered back. "Just let me get my coat."

She didn't even try to find Walt or Olivia to say good-night.

Seeing the garbage truck in Walt's driveway, parked up against a huge pine tree, almost ruined her mood. If only Patrick had enough money to buy a "regular" car just for dates. But she knew he was saving every penny he earned toward buying a second truck.

33

This is *not* smart, she told herself as Patrick climbed in beside her, saying only, "Mary Ellen," before taking her in his arms.

There were only two situations in Mary Ellen's life when she felt totally, completely happy. The first was leading the cheering at a winning Tarenton game. The second was kissing Patrick Henley.

She had kissed other boys: Troy; Donny; and, more often, Pres. Sometimes because it was expected and sometimes because she felt like it. She liked kissing. But kissing Patrick was different. It was, she was positive, the reason kissing had been invented in the first place, so that when you felt something so strong for someone, you could express how you felt.

She loved being close to Patrick. But it was hard to be careful about her feelings. When it was cold and dark outside and the two of them were alone together, the warmth of his closeness began to melt away her resistance.

Tight in Patrick's arms, his lips on hers, she began to float away on her own feelings and the strength of Patrick's feelings.

But whatever else Mary Ellen Kirkwood knew, she knew that the one thing she could not do was give in to the demands of her own body, no matter how much she wanted to. And she *did* want to.

Feeling her determination oozing away in the heat of Patrick's kisses, she used a trick she'd used before: She forced into her mind the image of Patrick in his coveralls, Patrick collecting garbage, Patrick emptying the cans into the truck.

It worked, as it always did.

"Patrick, no!" she whispered now, pushing him away as she always did.

Patrick had been expecting it. He wasn't disappointed. The last thing in the world he wanted was a purely physical relationship with Mary Ellen. What he really wanted was for her to say, "I love you, Patrick, and I don't care *what* you do for a living!"

But he knew she wasn't about to say that, any more than she was about to give in to any physical demands made on her if they didn't fit in with her plans.

"It's late, Patrick," she said weakly, breathing hard, moving as far away from him as possible. The door handle jabbed into her side.

"Mary Ellen," Patrick said wearily, leaning back against the seat, "when are you just going to give it up and admit that you're nuts about me?"

"I'm sorry," she said meekly, surprising him. Mary Ellen was many things, but meek had never been one of them. "But I can't. . . ."

"Can't what? Can't *what*? Can't be seen publicly with a garbage collector? That's all it is, and you know it. You know how I feel about you, and you feel the same way about me. You just won't admit it. One of these days, Mary Ellen. . . ."

But he gave up and took her home.

That was one thing about Patrick, Mary Ellen thought as she climbed down out of the truck, he had too much pride to force himself on any girl.

That thought was immediately followed by the

more disquieting one that Patrick Henley didn't *need* to force himself on anyone. There was a line of Tarenton girls as long as the Amazon River hungering for Patrick. He wouldn't hang around forever, waiting for Mary Ellen Kirkwood to fall into his arms and stay there.

It always amazed her that he hadn't given up on her long ago. And, she thought as she went into the house, smiling, it delighted her.

Olivia had been grounded. Probably forever, she thought grimly, as she entered the gym for a practice session Saturday afternoon. The scene with her mother last night had been a real dilly.

"All those years of standing by your hospital bed and this is how you pay me back? By poisoning your body with liquor?"

Olivia groaned. She had a killer of a headache, with little blue and black dots dancing before her eyes; her mother had continued the lecture throughout breakfast; and worst of all, Olivia was very fuzzy on the details of what had happened the night before.

There had been this guy . . . Walt had been furious. And Vanessa . . . Vanessa was there. What was Vanessa doing there?

Whatever it was, Olivia knew, if Vanessa was involved, it hadn't been good. Any chance she got to make trouble for the cheerleaders, she took.

Mary Ellen, Nancy, Walt, and Pres, wearing sweat clothes, were already doing warm-up exercises. Angie hadn't appeared yet and Ardith Engborg had just come into the gym.

But Olivia was interested only in Walt. This whole thing was just so silly and stupid. They had a great thing going and they both knew it. Each of them had said at least a hundred times, "I didn't know how nice it could be to have someone."

Walt couldn't possibly let a silly little thing like that business last night ruin everything. She just needed to talk to him, that was all. Walt wasn't stupid. She could make him understand.

She just wished she understood it better herself.

Before she reached the others, Ardith Engborg called out in a cold, clear voice, "Olivia? My office, please. Now!"

Olivia's nerves, already strained, shrieked in protest, Oh, no! How had she found out already? And the answer came to her instantly: Vanessa. She'd tattled to Daddy, and the superintendent of schools had then called Ardith Engborg so fast the telephone wires had probably sizzled.

Walt flushed a deep red and carefully studied the floor. The others exchanged knowing glances.

They all know, Olivia thought, horribly embarrassed. They probably know more about what happened last night than I do.

Without looking at anyone, Olivia continued on across the gym floor, feeling very, very small.

Angie came bouncing in through the gym doors and hurried over to the others, calling out, "Hi, guys! What's going — oh . . . ," as she spotted Olivia walking toward Mrs. Engborg. "Oh-oh."

The lecture Olivia got from her coach was

worse than the one her mother had delivered. Her mother was always expecting stupid things from her daughter, whom she still saw as an invalid, one who needed to be sheltered from the outside world. Even something as minor as leaving for school in the morning without an umbrella ("They mentioned rain in the forecast last night,") was seen as a stupid action on Olivia's part.

But Mrs. Engborg had expected only good things from her, as she did from all of the squad members, and Olivia felt the woman's disappointment keenly.

"I have every right to remove you from the squad, Olivia," she said, sitting on her desk as Olivia stood by the door, her hands clasped in front of her. "The rules state very clearly that one of the grounds for dismissal is 'any behavior inappropriate for an officer representing the school.' Getting drunk and making a spectacle of yourself at a party attended by many of your classmates certainly fits that category, doesn't it?"

Olivia nodded, miserable. She'd let Mrs. Engborg down, let the squad down, let the whole school down.

"You were wearing your uniform, too, weren't you? Which means that even those guests at the party who didn't know you, knew you represented Tarenton.

"I should suspend you. You know that. If I didn't feel that it would affect the entire squad adversely, I would do just that. But it doesn't seem fair to punish them and, indirectly, the whole school, by creating a lot of unpleasant

38

gossip just because *you* behaved badly."

Olivia stood silently, her heart pounding. If Coach suspended her, the entire school would know what she'd done, her mother would never let her hear the last of it, and worst of all, Walt would never, ever speak to her again. Ever.

"So I'm giving you a warning this time, Olivia. But pay attention to it. If I ever hear so much as the slightest hint that you've done anything like this again, I won't even stop to ask questions. Do you understand?"

Olivia nodded, breathing a huge sigh of relief. She'd been given a second chance.

"I promise," she told Mrs. Engborg gratefully. "I'll never do anything so stupid again. And . . . thanks!"

Mrs. Engborg nodded curtly. "Now we're due at that practice session. It won't be easy for you, with the headache you must have right about now, but the exercise will do you good. Come on, the others are waiting."

The others. Including Walt, Olivia thought, all nerves again as they left the office. Mrs. Engborg is keeping me on as a cheerleader. Is Walt going to be as forgiving and keep me on as his girl friend? He has to. He just has to! she vowed as she walked into the gym, feeling everyone's eyes on her. I have to *make* him forgive me.

But, seeing the cold, grim expression on Walt's round face as she approached the group, she wasn't at all sure she was going to be as lucky with Walt as she'd been with Ardith Engborg.

CHAPTER

The others had watched Olivia disappear after Mrs. Engborg. They stared at each other in dismay.

Pres shrugged. "So she had one too many. Big deal."

Walt reddened but said nothing. He busied himself with his sneaker laces.

"Poor Olivia," Angie said, but Nancy Goldstein made a face.

"I thought it was all pretty disgusting," she said, watching Walt fumble with his shoes. "Getting drunk was bad enough. But a hot necking session with someone you're not even going with . . . that's just plain stupid!"

Mary Ellen flushed, remembering the few delicious moments with Patrick in his truck. *Stupid*, huh? Well, she'd known *that* at the time. But it certainly hadn't felt stupid. It had felt . . . wonderful. So there, Nancy Goldstein!

Pres, watching Mary Ellen's face, knew she'd

been with Patrick Henley. He'd seen them leave the party together and the look on her face now told him what he'd suspected for a long time: Mary Ellen was really crazy about Patrick.

But she'd never admit it. Pres knew that. Patrick didn't have the one thing Mary Ellen needed most: money. Or power. But then, money *was* power, wasn't it? Pres's father, Preston Tilford II, president of Tarenton Fabricators, certainly thought so. And so did Mary Ellen.

Pres did a series of leg stretches, flicking his eyes every now and then back to Mary Ellen. She really was beautiful. She looked like she belonged in a magazine or a movie, and there had been times when he'd found her very exciting. But he had no intention of being used or manipulated.

The funny thing was, he thought, stretching his hamstrings, Mary Ellen's ambitions had always kept her emotions under control. And yet Kerry, who wasn't the least bit ambitious, was doing just as great a job of telling him *no* at crucial moments as Mary Ellen ever had.

Maybe it's just me, he thought dryly. Maybe it's my deodorant or my breath. Maybe I'm just not sexy enough. He was still smiling at such a ridiculous notion when Mrs. Engborg and Olivia returned to the group.

A very pale Olivia took her place on the gym floor without a word to anyone. During the remainder of the warm-up session and the practice following, she kept glancing over at Walt. He refused to look at her.

When Mrs. Engborg asked the two of them

41

to do a Side Thigh Sit, Walt couldn't very well refuse. But his arm around her waist was rigid, his smile forced and phony. He held her as if she had some terrible disease he was afraid of catching. His obvious reluctance to work with her made her feel worse than his anger the night before. Even if he didn't forgive her (but of course he would), and refused to date her anymore (but of course he wouldn't), they still *had* to be able to work together on the squad. One of Mrs. Engborg's cardinal rules was: Don't let your personal problems interfere with your cheering. Had Walt forgotten that?

Walt hadn't forgotten that. He simply couldn't shake the image of Olivia sitting on that creep's lap, kissing him as if she was resuscitating him. It disgusted him. If it had been Mary Ellen, well, that would have been no surprise to anyone. Not that she was a tramp — she wasn't. She was just a lot more casual about things like that, especially at parties.

But Olivia *wasn't*. At least, not the Olivia Walt had thought he knew so well. And loved.

And although his eyes never met hers during practice, he did sneak a peek at her more than once. Each time, the sight of her tiny, delicate body flying through the air, the reddish tint in her light brown hair shining under the lights overhead, made his heart feel as if someone was squeezing it.

In a million years, Walt would never have dreamed that someone as sweet and shy and smart as Olivia would love him. He wasn't good-looking like Patrick Henley or Pres, and he certainly wasn't as smart as Patrick or as rich as Pres.

And then when she *did* love him, he never would have dreamed that someone as sweet and shy and smart as Olivia would stab him right through the heart the way she had.

I should have known better, he thought bitterly as the whistle blew to end the session. I should have known it was too good to be true. Why would someone like Olivia stick with someone like me?

She had said she loved him. But if you loved someone, you don't do what she'd done. *Do* you?

No, he thought grimly, heading for the boys' locker room.

When Olivia caught up with him and faced him, whispering, "Walt, please can't we talk?" he could only look over her head and say, "I'm in a hurry. Excuse me," and walk away from her.

"You're being a real jerk," Pres said abruptly, as Walt came out of the shower later, his wet, wavy hair curling about his round face.

Walt flushed and fumbled in his gym bag for his comb. "Stay out of it, Pres. You don't know anything about it."

"Sure, I do." Pres stood at the mirror, brushing his own sleek dark-blond hair. "She had a drink or two and it sandbagged her."

"No, *she* sandbagged *me*," Walt said harshly, pulling on a pair of jeans and a sweatshirt.

"Not on purpose," Pres said easily, trying to get his hair to lie just right. "She wasn't really operating with all four cylinders. Know what I mean?"

Walt gave Pres's reflection in the mirror a disgusted look and said, "She's not a car, Pres!"

A shrug. "Women, cars, what's the difference?" Pres answered, feeling only a slight twinge of disloyalty to Kerry. "Sometimes their engines purr, which is good. But sometimes they give you trouble, which is not good. You gotta learn to take the bad with the good, Walt, my boy."

Walt zipped up his gym bag and picked up his jacket. "No," he said to Pres's back. "No, that's where you're wrong. I don't *gotta* do anything. As far as I'm concerned, that creep can have Olivia. They deserve each other."

And he turned and left.

Pres figured Walt just didn't feel like talking about it anymore. Which was all right with him, because the last thing he wanted to be was Mr. Lonelyhearts. He had troubles of his own. If he had to take one more cold shower after a date with Kerry, his skin was going to jump right off his body and run away.

The truth was, Walt left because the more he thought about Olivia and that guy, the more he felt like crying. And he'd cut out his heart before he'd let himself do something like that in front of cool, smooth Pres.

In the girls' locker room, Mary Ellen said, "I don't see what Walt is making such a big fuss about. I mean, it's not like you ran off with that guy, whoever he was. And it was a *party*, for Pete's sake!"

Olivia would have been grateful for the support if it hadn't come from Mary Ellen. Unfortunately, she'd always thought her team captain was a little flighty and far too shallow. The remarks would have meant more coming from Nancy.

But the only thing she got from Nancy was a cool, "Well, you'd better straighten things out with Walt, because what this squad doesn't need is two people who can't stand each other."

"I know that!" Olivia cried, tears of frustration springing into her eyes. "I tried, but he won't talk to me!"

It was Angie who put her arm around Olivia's shoulders and said soothingly, "He will. I know he will. You'll make up. Walt's crazy about you. He'll get over this, you wait and see."

Angie always expects everything to turn out perfectly, Mary Ellen thought, watching the two of them. I wonder if she ever read anything but fairy tales when she was little?

After a thoroughly rotten afternoon, Olivia had to endure a continuation of her mother's lecture on the perils of drinking, during the drive home. If only she had her own license, her mother wouldn't have to pick her up and take her places. One nice thing about dating Walt had been going somewhere in a car without her mother yammering away at her.

"Mother, I *said* I was sorry," Olivia said, wondering if her mother had ever been young herself. Probably not. Most likely she'd just appeared one day, a full-grown adult ready to marry and have a child to nag to death. "What else can I say? You've already grounded me. Can't we just forget it now?"

"Forget it? *Forget it?* You go out and make a total fool of yourself . . ."

And on and on and on. Olivia had learned long ago that the best way to get through her mother's lectures and speeches was to simply tune her out. She had worked hard at developing the knack of looking reasonably attentive while her mind went elsewhere. And she had succeeded.

Right now, her mind was on Walt.

". . . and when I think of what we went through just trying to keep you alive, and you think nothing of pouring that poison into your body . . ."

He wasn't going to let her apologize. He'd made that crystal clear. With the rest of the squad watching and listening, he'd made it plain that he wanted nothing more to do with her. How could he be so cruel?

". . . seem to be the only one who cares about what happens to you. You certainly don't . . ."

Olivia had almost no experience with the opposite sex and she really didn't know what to do about Walt. Should she push? Should she try harder to get him to listen to her? If you really loved someone and you'd done something to hurt him, are you supposed to hang in there until you can make things right? For how long?

". . . lucky you didn't fall and crack your head or . . ."

How were you supposed to know when to give up on someone? She certainly couldn't ask her mother.

". . . your body is a temple and if you won't take care of it, who . . ."

46

The minute she got in the house, Olivia escaped to her room.

". . . not one foot outside this house . . ." floated up the stairs after her, like poisonous gas.

Walt was in his room, sitting on the braided rug staring at Olivia's picture, when she called. His first instinct was to hang up, but he fought that impulse. The sound of her voice was too tempting. Besides, he was curious. What could she possibly say? He'd caught her in the act, hadn't he? But he'd stay on the line long enough to hear her stupid excuses.

She didn't make any excuses. She just said she was sorry and asked him to please, at least, *talk* to her.

He wanted to. More than anything. More than anything except . . . holding on to his pride. He couldn't do it. He already missed Olivia terribly. He felt as if some really important part of him had been amputated.

But this was Walt's first encounter with love, too, and he didn't know any more about it than she did. If he forgave her, wouldn't she think he was a fool? Wouldn't she think he was a real pushover? And if she thought that, then she'd think she could do the same kind of thing at parties any time she felt like it.

And everybody at school would see what a stupid fool he was! No wonder he had to work so hard at getting good grades. No wonder it had been so easy for Olivia to make him look stupid — he *was* stupid! If he wasn't, how could he even think about just forgetting the whole thing, the way she wanted him to?

"You're wasting your time," he said coldly, gripping the receiver so tightly his knuckles turned white. "If you want someone to talk to, why don't you call the creep you were glued to last night? I'm sure he'd be real happy to listen to you . . . and more than that."

He slammed the phone into its cradle. Olivia had no way of knowing he had tears in his eyes.

And so did she. Hurt and angry, she sat silently for a few minutes. She thought about the joy of cheerleading, the glorious feeling of getting out there in front of the whole school, knowing she looked pretty in her bright red and white uniform, and cheering the team on to victory or supporting the guys when they lost. It was . . . it was feeling like a *part* of something important that she loved the most. And getting caught up in the excitement and fears and hopes of a whole group, working as one. It was so different from sitting alone in her room.

She lay on the floor, staring up at the ceiling. They were all so different, the six of them on Varsity. Yet, when they got out there on the floor in their uniforms, they worked together like one.

Except when there was a serious problem somewhere on the squad.

Like now, she thought, rolling over onto her stomach. Walt and I have a serious problem and it's going to affect the whole squad . . . unless he forgives me. And he certainly doesn't sound as if he's even thinking about it.

I'd forgive *him*, she thought angrily. I would! Because I love him. Maybe he doesn't love me at all, not really. Maybe he never did.

By the time the telephone rang, she was totally disgusted with Walt. So when the voice belonging to Boomer said, "Hi, there! This is Boomer, the guy you met last night at the party? How about we get together tonight?" Olivia said yes.

She regretted it immediately but it was too late. She couldn't very well hang up now. Besides, since everybody thought she was such a jerk, she obviously belonged with another jerk. At least *somebody* wanted her, even if Walt didn't.

She told Boomer it would have to be late when she met him, because she had to study first. The truth was, she was going to have to sneak out of the house, and it wouldn't be easy. She was grateful for two things: Her parents always went to bed early, and their house had a back staircase. It creaked, but it was on the opposite side of the house from the bedrooms.

She'd manage to get out somehow. She couldn't sit in this house all night feeling sorry for herself. She arranged to meet Boomer a block from her house at ten-thirty, and hung up. He sounded very pleased.

Maybe he would even shave.

CHAPTER

While Olivia was sitting in her bedroom listening for the sounds of her parents retiring for the night, her teammates, with the exception of Walt Manners, were gathered at Nancy Goldstein's house, discussing the latest crisis involving Tarenton's Varsity Cheerleaders. Even Pres was there on a Saturday night, only because Kerry was away at her grandparents' for the weekend.

"It's not going to be so easy for Walt to forgive Olivia," Nancy said, sitting on the fireplace hearth beside Josh Breitman, her boyfriend. Nancy and Josh had "discovered" each other during a brief period when Josh had temporarily taken Pres's place on the squad. Their parents, who were best friends, were almost as thrilled with the relationship as their offspring were.

"Oh, Nancy, don't be so pompous!" Mary Ellen said in disgust. She was sitting on the floor, a bowl of popcorn propped between her jean-clad legs. Still frustrated about having to refuse the modeling job, she had no patience with Nancy's lack of understanding. "Haven't you ever in your life done anything stupid and been sorry for it afterwards?"

Dumb question, Mary Ellen admitted to herself.

Nancy thought about her brief romance with Ben Adamson, but she didn't regret it. She remembered the excitement, clearly.

Nancy looked blank. "The thing is," she said after a moment, "if they don't make up right away, the whole squad is going to suffer."

"*So* are Walt and Olivia," Angie said sadly.

"Well, *I* know that! I'm worried about them, too, just as much as you are. But we represent the whole school, not just two people."

Mary Ellen muttered, "Oh, brother," under her breath, but Pres jumped in with, "Look, why don't we do like they do in the movies? We'll get them together and then leave them alone so they have to hash it all out."

"That's a great idea, Pres!" Angie cried.

Mary Ellen wasn't so sure. "How do we know they'll come? Walt didn't seem at all keen on even speaking to Olivia."

"No problem. They should be here anyway, shouldn't they? The only reason they aren't is that we wanted to talk about them, see what we could figure out. Well, we *did* that. So now we call Walt and tell him we're having a meeting and to get right over here, and then we do the same with Olivia. Then when they get here, we all split!"

"Oh, right," Nancy said sarcastically, "so they

conduct World War III right here in the Goldstein living room. My mother's going to be just wild about that idea!"

"*Nancy!*" Mary Ellen yelled.

"Okay, okay, I give up. Go ahead and call them. I'll just get busy moving all the breakables into the hall closet."

Pres laughed and went to the phone. He called Walt first. "No problem," he said as he hung up. "He'll be right over."

"And did you tell him Olivia was going to be here?" Nancy asked sweetly.

Pres looked at her. "Are you kidding? Anyway, he didn't ask."

"I'll call Olivia," Angie offered.

But the call to Olivia turned out differently. Angie turned away from the phone with disappointment on her face. "She can't come," she told the others. "She's been grounded. She's only allowed out for games and practice sessions."

"Oh, great!" Pres groaned. "Now we've got Walt and no Olivia. What good is that going to do?"

"Well, it was *your* idea," Nancy accused.

Angie, as always, tried to smooth the whole thing over by pointing out that they really hadn't *told* Walt that Olivia would be there. But they all knew he probably expected her to be.

"Nancy," Josh asked suddenly as they all sat there, lost in thought, "can I talk to you for a sec?"

Everyone looked at him. Nancy frowned. "Oh . . . well, sure."

He led the way into the dining room. "Listen,"

he said earnestly, leaning against the table, "I think I should split. I mean, this is private stuff, cheerleader stuff. I really don't belong here."

Nancy's mouth dropped open. She stared up into his broad, pleasant face. "Josh, what are you talking about? You know all about the squad."

He shook his dark, curly head. "Yeah, I know. But I'm not *on* the squad anymore."

She reached up and touched his cheek with her hand. "You're being silly. Of course you belong here. Anyway, this is my house. I want you here. And so do the others. Now c'mon."

Sighing, he followed her back into the living room. But he was quiet the rest of the night.

The minute she'd hung up on Angie, Olivia was sorry. She should have gone. Walt was probably there. Maybe. . . .

Then she remembered the look on Walt's face, heard him say again, "Excuse me, I'm in a hurry," and was glad she'd said no.

Besides, of all of them, only Angie had been supportive. Sitting in a room with all of them, feeling their disapproval, their hostility toward her for the trouble she had caused in the squad, would be about as much fun as doing a cartwheel wearing a pair of skis. Now all she had to do was figure out how to get out of the house by ten-twenty or so.

It was easier than she thought it would be.

Her mother, saying plaintively that she was exhausted by the "emotional strain" of what she termed "my daughter's disgraceful behavior," took to her bed before ten o'clock. Olivia's father followed minutes later.

Hardly able to believe her good luck, Olivia was still not taking any chances. Trying out something she'd seen on television, she shoved her pillows this way and that under her blankets until it looked as if there might be a body in there. Eventually, she got the effect she wanted.

The most difficult part was getting out of her own bedroom and past her parents' room, which was right next to hers (an arrangement Olivia detested).

She waited as long as she possibly could before leaving her room, wearing only knee-hi's on her feet, carrying her boots in her hand. She closed her bedroom door so gently the knob didn't even click. Listening at her parents' bedroom door, she heard nothing. Not a murmur, not a sound.

So far, so good.

The stairs did *not* creak, partly because she tiptoed down them by placing a foot on the far side of each stair instead of in the middle, balancing her weight carefully.

I'd make a good burglar, she thought, trying not to giggle.

Don't get cocky, Olivia, she warned herself as she made her way through the kitchen to the back door. It was locked, of course, but she knew the lockset was much quieter than the one on the front door.

She made it outside without a sound. The sidewalk was cold on her stocking feet, but her boots had heels and made too much noise to put on just yet. All the way down the street, she kept expecting to hear her mother's voice shrieking out the bedroom window, "Olivia Evans, you get back here this instant, do you *hear* me?"

Probably followed by, "It is a freezing cold night and you will catch your death of pneumonia!"

Pneumonia was one of her mother's favorites. Olivia had never in her life known anyone who actually caught pneumonia — even though she knew plenty of people who didn't dress properly in cold weather, got their feet wet when it rained, didn't get enough sleep, and never ate properly.

But her mother seemed to believe pneumonia was lurking around every corner, carried in every breeze that blew.

Well, it *was* cold out. But her turtleneck sweater, pile-lined jacket, and jeans were plenty warm enough, and her fur-lined boots, when she slipped into them, kept her feet warm. No pneumonia tonight.

Boomer was right on time, whizzing around the corner in a tired old sedan badly rusted around the edges, screeching to a stop in front of Olivia. He didn't even open the door for her, just sat there, engine idling roughly, waiting for her to get in.

She did, wondering as she yanked the door open and slid into the front seat, what on earth she was doing.

When Walt walked into Nancy's living room and saw everyone but Olivia there, his disappointment was much stronger than his relief.

"So . . . what's going on?" he asked, his eyebrows lifting.

Left with no excuse for calling him in the first place, everyone looked blank.

Mary Ellen thought faster than anyone else. "Well," she said brightly, "we thought we'd all go out for pizza. Knowing how you feel about pizza, we couldn't very well leave you out, could we?"

And if he swallows that, she thought to herself, then this business with Olivia has really drilled a hole in his brain.

Walt bought it. He was getting too depressed, anyway, sitting on the floor of his room staring at Olivia's picture, and if anything could snap him out of that, it would be food.

Besides, these were his friends. They knew what had happened and they understood how he felt. Even Pres must have thought about how *he'd* feel if he'd caught Kerry with another guy.

"Sounds great!" Walt said heartily. "I'm starving." He forced a laugh. "So what else is new, right? C'mon, let's go!"

Just about the time Walt was deciding that going out wasn't a bad idea, Olivia was deciding just the opposite. Only it was too late to change her mind. Boomer had a definite talent for driving with his left hand and using his right to seek out Olivia's knee. She kept brushing it away and he kept putting it back. Music blared from the car radio, and Boomer was driving much too fast.

I need to have my head examined, she thought.

"Where are we going in such a hurry?" she shouted over the wailing of a woman whose heart had been broken by a "hard-drinkin' man."

"Lookout Point," he shouted back.

Oh-oh. Well, what had she expected after last night (which she was just now beginning to remember with sickening clarity)? She shuddered.

"Look," she said loudly, moving closer to him, "I'm starving. I didn't have any dinner." (Which was true enough — how could she eat with her mother's accusing eyes pinned on her face?) "Can't we go get something to eat?"

"No can do," Boomer said, his hand once again locating her knee. "The wallet is flat, know what I'm saying? Flat like a pancake. No bucks, no food, that's the way the world works, honey."

"Oh, that's okay," she said quickly. "Money's no problem. I've got money."

He looked over at her with interest. "Yeah? And you don't mind sharing it with old Boomer here? Hey, that's real sweet, honey. I finally got me a liberated woman."

She removed his hand from her knee.

"Okay," he said. "Tell the truth, I didn't have much chow myself. What'll it be? Steak and fries? Hamburgers? Pizza?"

She tried to figure out quickly which would take the longest to cook and the longest to eat. Pizza?

"Pizza!" she answered, and he obligingly turned the car around to head for the pizza parlor.

Great. By the time they'd have finished eating,

she'd figure out a way to escape from this octopus. A headache? Stomachache? A sudden case of rabies? She'd think of something.

She just hoped he could keep his hands off her in the restaurant. She'd already made a fool of herself in public once this week. She wasn't shooting for twice.

Maybe Boomer, underneath all that groping, was a really intelligent person and a great conversationalist. After all, she really hadn't given him a chance yet. He'd gone to college. Surely there must be dozens of things he liked to talk about.

No such luck. The only subjects Boomer seemed to be interested in were biology, anatomy, and physics, his current experiment in physics involving the question of just how close two people could sit in a restaurant without actually suffocating each other.

The pizza place was crowded, as it always was on Saturday night, and Olivia could feel a lot of eyes on her. She knew people were wondering what Olivia Evans was doing with some tall, skinny guy in jeans and a sweater with a hole in the elbow, which he'd obviously used to clean the engine of his sedan. And where, the eyes on her seemed to ask accusingly, was Walt Manners?

A question that was answered just as Boomer planted a very intense kiss on Olivia's mouth.

Because that was the moment when the other five members of the Tarenton Varsity Cheerleading Squad walked through the front door of the restaurant in which Boomer was kissing Olivia. Walt Manners was leading the pack.

The very first thing he saw when he walked through the door was Olivia, being kissed very thoroughly by the same person she'd been kissing the night before.

Pres thought, Oh no!

Mary Ellen thought, Why, that little fox! What is she up to?

Nancy turned away, thoroughly disgusted, and Angie said in a whisper, "But I thought . . . I thought she was grounded!"

And Olivia, who only closed her eyes when she was kissing someone she really cared about, stared at them from behind Boomer's shoulder.

CHAPTER

Walt turned to leave, but Pres stopped him.

"Take it easy," he said, blocking Walt's way. "Stay cool. We came here to get pizza and pizza is what we're going to get."

Angie couldn't believe her eyes. Olivia had said on the phone that she'd been grounded. Angie had believed her. Now she knew why Olivia had lied.

"Maybe she *didn't* lie," Mary Ellen said, as they found an empty booth and squeezed into it. Mary Ellen, taking advantage of Kerry's temporary absence, made sure she sat beside Pres. "Maybe she *was* grounded. Maybe she sneaked out."

"She lives in a two-story house," Walt said bitterly, staring at Olivia's back. "How do you sneak out of a two-story house when your bedroom isn't on the ground floor? Especially when your mother has the eyes of a hawk, and ears that can hear a piece of string hit the floor?"

He tried to keep his eyes off Olivia and the guy she was with. He felt as if he'd fallen into an abandoned well. It was a very dark, cold place to be.

If Walt hadn't been so lost in self-pity and hurt and anger, he might have noticed that Olivia looked extremely uncomfortable and unhappy with her date.

She never even touched the pizza. "Okay, more for me!" Boomer said happily, and inhaled the entire pie in less than five minutes.

"Can we go, please?" Olivia begged, feeling Walt's eyes on the back of her head.

If she hadn't pointedly handed Boomer a paper napkin, she was sure he wouldn't even have wiped the tomato sauce from his mouth and chin.

She couldn't for the life of her remember why she had agreed to even be on the same planet with this person, let alone sit in a public place with him. And how was she going to talk him out of Lookout Point?

Well, she wasn't, as it turned out. She tried. But he just upped the volume on the car radio to drown out her complaints about a headache and a stomachache and how late it was and she was awfully cold and her parents would be worried and. . . .

Boomer sped on up the hill.

Olivia and Walt had been to Lookout Point only once or twice. But Olivia knew perfectly well what the clearing at the top of the little hill was for. This, she thought grimly as Boomer pulled the old sedan to a halt under a group of pine trees, is where all those girls I hear about at school get "into trouble."

But all those girls were safe at home tonight, because Boomer's car, she noticed unhappily, was the only one there. What if she needed help?

After all, she knew perfectly well that Boomer had every right to expect her full cooperation, after her behavior at the party and the way she'd jumped at his invitation tonight.

Help, she wailed silently. Somebody get me out of this and I promise I'll never do anything this stupid again! *Never!*

She wished with all her heart that last night had never happened, that she'd never met this person beside her, and, most of all, that she was back at the pizza place, sitting beside Walt just like always, his arm around her shoulders, holding her close.

There was an arm around her, all right, but it wasn't Walt's. And in no time at all, there were *two* arms around her, both clutching, grabbing, and groping. A mouth smelling strongly of pizza landed on hers. There was no question about its determination. And there was no question about the intent of all those hands pulling and tugging at her clothes.

For the first time since her last surgery as a child, Olivia Evans was thoroughly frightened. She was totally alone out in the middle of nowhere, and the person with her was determined to take something from her that she wasn't willing to give. Certainly not to *him*!

Frantic, she began struggling, only to realize a second later that trying to fight him off was only increasing his determination. She'd heard about guys like that.

She wouldn't have thought someone so skinny could be so strong.

"Please!" she gasped, pulling her head away with great effort. "Please, don't!"

He laughed, and it was not a nice sound. "Hey, what is this?" he said harshly. "You're not one of those high school teases, are you? Man, I can't stand girls like that!"

"No, no," she said quickly, "I'm not! Last night ... well, I was drunk. I'm sorry if I gave you the wrong idea. Really, I am."

He laughed again, reaching for her. "You didn't give me the wrong idea, honey. You gave me the *right* idea!"

And he was at her again, his hands beginning the Grand Tour.

She had to *do* something. I can't just sit here and let this happen, she thought desperately. It can't be like this. Not with *him*! Anger came next. He has no right to do this, she thought furiously, no right at all. Just because I'm smaller than he is. . . .

His hands were under her coat, when she remembered her purse. The large leather shoulder bag contained, somewhere deep inside it, the small but fairly heavy metal thermos she always carried to practice sessions. She'd been so upset when she got home that she'd forgotten to take it out. Because she hadn't felt like eating or drinking anything all day, it was still full of juice.

Wouldn't the juice give the metal thermos even more of a wallop?

Olivia Evans had suffered so much pain as a child, that she could not even bring herself to swat a fly. She had never in her life caused physical pain to any human being. But it was crystal-clear to Olivia at that moment that if she didn't do something to stop Boomer, he was going to make it impossible for her to ever face Walt again. And impossible for her to face her-*self*.

She couldn't let that happen. She hadn't fought for her life in all those hospital beds only to have some jerk with pizza breath ruin it for her now.

Wrenching her right arm free, she grabbed the shoulder bag in her right hand, drew her arm backwards as far as her shoulder joint would allow, and in one vigorous swoop of her arm, brought the shoulder bag with its juice-filled thermos down against Boomer's face with every ounce of strength she had left in her.

She heard the glass liner shatter inside the thermos as Boomer shrieked. More surprised than hurt, he let go of her. In that split second, as his hands released her and went to his face, she lunged for the door handle, shoved the door open, and threw her body out of the car.

She was off and running into the woods before he'd finished checking his face for blood.

If there hadn't been a moon, Olivia would have fallen a hundred times before she made it to the highway. But there was, and because it was nearly full, it was almost as effective as a flashlight. Still, the woods were unfamiliar to her. By the time she stumbled out of the woods at the edge of the highway, her hair was full of brambles, her face scratched, and her bruised knees were poking through the jeans ripped by more than one fall.

She was afraid to walk along the highway. Boomer could come along at any second. So she stayed along the edge of the woods, ducking behind a pine tree every few minutes to check out the road alongside her.

She hadn't been walking long when she spotted two sets of headlights at the same time. One set came toward her from town, the other came from Lookout Point. She'd know the sound of that engine anywhere. Boomer must be furious with her. If he found her now. . . .

She shuddered, and made a split-second decision.

Jumping out into the middle of the road directly in the path of the vehicle coming from town, she waved her arms frantically, forcing it to screech to a halt. Blinded by the headlights, she didn't realize until she ran to the passenger's side, that it was a truck.

A garbage truck.

It was Patrick Henley's garbage truck, and Patrick was driving it.

"Olivia! What the hell —" he cried as she yanked the door open.

Sobbing with relief, she climbed up into the seat of the cab just as Boomer's old sedan arrived on the spot. It slowed down, almost came to a stop, and then Boomer stepped on the gas and roared away.

Olivia, her face streaked with tears, her hair a wild tangle, her clothes in disarray, slammed the door shut, and sat there for a second, breathing heavily. Then she turned to Patrick, whose mouth was open in disbelief, and with tears in her eyes and the tiniest smile, said, "Hi. Am I too late for the garbage?"

He threw his head back and laughed.

"Could we just go, Patrick?" she asked quickly. "I mean, wherever you're going is just fine. I just . . . well, I don't think it's a good idea to hang around here, okay?"

"I'm on my way to the dump," he said, putting the truck in gear and starting down the highway. "It's at the far end of this road. I pick up late on Saturdays, because that's when people clean out their attics and garages. I like to get in on that."

Then he glanced over at her and asked, "You okay?"

She nodded.

"That the same guy you were with last night?"

She couldn't stop crying. Nodding, she said between sobs, "Patrick, how many different ways are there to be stupid?"

He laughed. "Well, let me put it this way. I've never known anyone in my whole life who hasn't done at least one really stupid thing, and most of them, including yours truly here, have done quite a few stupid things."

Not my mother, Olivia thought, wiping her nose with her jacket sleeve. My mother never does anything stupid!

Oh, yes, she does, a voice inside her said rudely. She had *you*, didn't she?

She groaned.

"You're not hurt, are you?" Patrick asked anxiously, slowing down. "I guess seeing you jump out at my truck that way made me think you were okay. I thought you were a deer at first."

"No, no, I'm fine," she assured him. She giggled. "I'm not too sure about him, though."

"Look, I'm sorry about the truck," he said, turning off onto a dirt road. Olivia saw a sign reading TARENTON CITY DUMP posted on a tree. "I mean, it being loaded like this. Usually, I only pick people up when I'm empty."

He glanced over at her, his expression serious. "But you didn't look like you could wait for my return trip."

"I couldn't have," Olivia agreed. "Besides, I don't see why Mary Ellen makes such a fuss about —"

She stopped, horrified. I can't believe I said that. "Oh, Patrick, I'm sorry!" she cried. "I —"

"It's okay," he said quickly, smiling at her. "Really. Everyone knows how Mary Ellen feels, including me. She's never made any secret of it. If she's not careful, she's going to put a permanent wrinkle in that beautiful nose of hers, just from every time she sees my truck.

"Anyway," he added as he pulled the truck to

a complete stop, "if my feelings got hurt that easily, I'd have given up on her a long time ago. I guess you noticed at the party last night that I sure haven't done that. Yet."

Olivia searched her memory. Had she seen Patrick and Mary Ellen together last night? She couldn't remember. I guess I was too busy to notice, she thought bitterly.

"Will you be okay here while I go check for a spot to dump?" Patrick asked before he got out.

"Oh, sure. Would it be easier if I got out, too?"

Patrick laughed. "No, hon, you stay put. It's the back of the truck that goes up in the air. The cab stays right where it is."

She wasn't frightened anymore, and sat quietly while he was gone.

He came right back. She watched him carefully, enjoying the sight of him expertly turning the truck, backing it up slowly, and operating the lever that emptied the dumpster.

Mary Ellen is crazy, she thought, surprising herself.

Well, the little voice inside her pointed out, what does that make *you*? How much time have you spent trying to get to know Patrick Henley? And why haven't you? the voice went on ruthlessly, as Patrick finished the dumping and turned the truck around to leave. You haven't because he hauls garbage, that's why you haven't. You and Mary Ellen are *both* snobs!

I am *not* a snob, Olivia defended herself silently.

Aloud she said, "Patrick, thank you for rescuing me. I don't know what I would have done if you hadn't come along."

"Forget it," he said, turning the truck onto the highway. "No big deal. Glad I was there."

And he wouldn't have been if he didn't collect garbage, the little voice persisted nastily. So much for your petty snobbery, Olivia!

CHAPTER

"I'm never going to get out of this town!" Mary Ellen cried, staring forlornly at her bank book.

"Sure you are, Mary Ellen," her younger sister Gemma said. "You're going to New York to be the best model ever!" She was sitting on her bed, reading the Sunday comics. She looked adoringly at her older sister with wide blue eyes. "You'll figure something out."

"Oh, sure," Mary Ellen snapped, "and how am I even going to *get* to New York? Fly?" She flapped her arms.

Her sister flushed.

"I'm sorry," Mary Ellen said, sighing and stroking the ends of her blonde ponytail, "it's not your fault I couldn't take that job at Marnie's. If it weren't for cheerleading. . . .'

Gemma looked shocked. "You can't give that up, Mary Ellen! It's too important."

"Yeah. Well, it sure isn't going to get me to New York."

But Gemma was right. She couldn't quit the squad. Especially right now, when it was all she had.

Pres hadn't been the least bit interested in her last night. It wasn't as though she hadn't tried. But the only female Pres was interested in these days was Kerry Elliott. Even when Kerry wasn't around.

The great Mary Ellen Kirkwood, she thought sarcastically, the girl so many Tarenton High School girls envy. Shows how much they know!

"I *hate* winter!" Mary Ellen shouted. "It's so long!"

"Mary Ellen," Gemma pointed out, giggling, "you're funny!"

Her sister grinned. "Oh, yeah? Tell you what . . . get dressed. We'll go outside and have a snowball fight, just like we used to. If you win, winter is the shortest season. But if I hit you more times than you hit me, and I *will*, it's the longest, and the dumbest, and the ickiest and —"

"Okay, okay, I get the point!" Gemma, delighted that Mary Ellen had decided to stop brooding, threw the comics aside and ran around the room gathering up clothes to put on. "You go ahead. I'll be right down."

Gemma won, which Mary Ellen figured made sense, since she didn't seem to be winning much of anything these days.

But it was fun, anyway. And her spirits had lifted a bit until she saw Vanessa Barlow's car pull up at the curb and stop.

"What on earth does she want?" Mary Ellen muttered as Vanessa got out and came toward them. "Maybe she found out I scared off her date the other night and she's here to put a hex on me."

"You did what?" Gemma asked, her mouth shaped in a surprised "O."

"Nothing. Shhh! What do you want, Vanessa? Aren't you lost? Or are you just slumming?"

"We don't live in a slum!" Gemma protested indignantly. "This is a nice neighborhood!" She looked around at the tired but neat little houses as if to get support from them.

Vanessa, smartly dressed as always in a ski sweater and matching pants Mary Ellen was sure had come from Marnie's, smiled at Gemma and said, "If your sister says you live in a slum, then that's where you live. She's older than you are."

It was one thing for Mary Ellen to criticize the neighborhood and the bright turquoise house the Kirkwoods owned. But it was a different matter when the words came from Vanessa's mouth.

"What do you *want*?" she repeated icily.

Vanessa smiled.

She looks too happy, Mary Ellen thought. That means trouble. Trouble is Vanessa's drug. She gets high on it, especially if it's trouble that's going to drag somebody else way down.

"I was just wondering if you'd seen Olivia," Vanessa said, looking at Mary Ellen with wide, innocent eyes.

She knows I scared off Dum-Dum the other

night, Mary Ellen thought with certainty. She's come to pay me back for that.

"Olivia doesn't live in this neighborhood. Her address is right there in the phone book along with everyone else's."

Something flickered in Vanessa's tiger eyes. "Oh, I know that. But she's not home. I called. Her mother said she had a special cheerleading practice."

Mary Ellen frowned. "We never have practice on Sundays."

"I know that, too. And anyway, Patrick Henley isn't a cheerleader."

Mary Ellen was thoroughly confused. "Patrick? What's Patrick got to do with anything?"

"Oh, they're together," Vanessa purred. "Mrs. Evans told me you had a special practice session. I needed to see Olivia, so I was on my way to school to catch her there, and I saw Olivia and Patrick down by the lake. Looking very cozy, I must say. Arm-in-arm and all that. They were walking along the path. Together. So I guess Olivia just lied to her mother so she could be with Patrick."

Mary Ellen stared at her. Olivia and Patrick?

"My goodness," Vanessa said, watching Mary Ellen's face carefully, "it's hard to keep up with that girl, isn't it? First Walt, then that strange person at the party the other night, and now our Patrick."

She turned to leave, and then turned back again. "Listen," she said, taking something out of her purse, "the reason I was looking for her is, she left her charge card at Marnie's the last time she was there. Else asked me if I would give it to her."

Mary Ellen wasn't thinking clearly. "Else? Who's Else?"

"Mrs. Gunderson, idiot! My boss!"

She said it with such self-importance, Mary Ellen had to bite her lip to keep from reaching out and grabbing a handful of Vanessa's dark, silky hair and pulling with both hands. Hard.

"Here," Vanessa said, holding out a piece of blue plastic, "you see Olivia more than I do. You're such good friends." She smiled, but the smile never reached her eyes. "How about if you give it to her, okay?"

So she had at least been telling the truth about the charge card. Mary Ellen took it without a word. But she had to be lying about Olivia and Patrick. Of course she was.

Vanessa left, and Mary Ellen and Gemma went inside. In their room, Gemma asked in a voice full of concern, "Mary Ellen, what's wrong? You look really strange. I didn't hear Vanessa say anything really awful. Did I miss something?"

Mary Ellen lay on her stomach on her bed, not answering her sister. If Olivia goes out with Patrick, she thought, she'll fall in love with him, Walt or no Walt. How could she help it?

Patrick had dated other girls. Lots of them. But Mary Ellen had never let it upset her, mostly because there *were* lots of them. Patrick never got involved. The only girl with whom he'd kept up a long relationship, even if it was in bits and pieces, was Mary Ellen Kirkwood.

But Olivia . . . she'd be a different story. She's pretty and bright and nice, she thought despairingly. And she's a cheerleader, too, so I can't even say that I'm more important than she is. Olivia just might be the one girl who could turn Patrick Henley's mind away from Mary Ellen for good.

She can't *have* him, Mary Ellen thought angrily. She can't!

"Mary Ellen," Gemma asked, coming over to stand beside her sister's bed, "was it what Vanessa said about Olivia and Patrick?"

No answer. Which Gemma knew *was* an answer.

She frowned. "But I thought you didn't like Patrick. You said —"

"I know what I said!" Mary Ellen snapped. "And I'd appreciate it if you'd just please mind your own business."

A minute later, she heard the door close after Gemma, heard her footsteps going down the stairs.

Regretting her rudeness but grateful for the solitude, Mary Ellen laid her chin on her panda bear Jujube's stomach and said out loud, "Vanessa's lying. I know she is. She found out about the stunt I pulled the other night at Walt's party and she's just trying to get even."

Comforted by that thought, she fell asleep.

But Vanessa wasn't lying.

The night before, Patrick and Olivia had discovered that they liked a lot of the same things. They found they could talk easily and at length about all sorts of things. They were comfortable with each other.

And because neither was stupid, each was aware that at least part of the reason they were so comfortable was that they both loved somebody else.

"Friends?" Patrick had asked Saturday night after checking to make sure the kitchen door was still unlocked so that Olivia could sneak back into her house.

"Friends," she whispered, "and thanks for everything."

"No problem. Listen, I wouldn't mind working on this friendship a little more tomorrow afternoon. You available?"

She was supposed to be grounded. But . . . she really wanted to spend some time with Patrick. He was the only person she knew right now who wasn't totally disgusted with her.

"I could meet you at the library tomorrow and we could go for a walk."

Now all she had to do was talk her mother into letting her out of the house.

She invented a "special" cheerleading practice session. It worked, because her mother had seen how badly they'd performed at the last game.

"I'll get a ride home with one of the kids," she told her mother when she dropped Olivia off at school Sunday afternoon.

Then she walked to the library, where Patrick was waiting. They decided to go down and walk along the lake. Which was where Vanessa spotted them.

Vanessa wasn't the only one who called the Evans home that day asking for Olivia. Walt Manners called, too.

And Walt knew perfectly well there was no "special" cheerleading practice.

Unwilling to blow the whistle on Olivia, he told her mother he'd missed the practice because of a bad headache and was just calling to find out from Olivia how it had been. His voice was very calm and casual, but inside, he was fuming. Olivia had lied to her mother. So she was obviously with that stupid jerk from the party again!

Well, what did you expect? a voice inside him asked. *You* wouldn't talk to her! You wouldn't even let her apologize.

I was going to, he defended himself. That's why I was calling her. To talk.

Actually, it went deeper than just the need to talk to her. He had called her because he really didn't think he could get through another day without her. He was too miserable.

He would have liked to talk to his parents after he found out that Olivia wasn't home, but as always on Sunday, the house was full of people. He didn't feel like joining in the fun. He couldn't help remembering that one of the reasons Olivia said she had turned to that jerk in the first place was that Walt had been off entertaining everybody. It would be a while before he'd feel like doing that again.

Every time he passed his mother she was surrounded by people. She'd give him a little wave and a vague smile, as though he looked familiar to her but she couldn't quite place him.

He spent the rest of the day in his room, calling himself names for being stupid enough to let someone as pretty, as nice, and as smart as Olivia get away from him. The last thought he had before he fell asleep on the floor, Olivia's picture in his hand, was, She doesn't love me anymore. And I don't blame her.

"I love Walt a lot," Olivia told Patrick as they walked along the lake, "but he's not being very understanding right now. He's so stubborn!"

It was a cold, gray, windy day and even though Patrick had a friendly arm around Olivia's shoulders, she was very cold. She'd have to go home soon and get warm, but she was reluctant to leave Patrick's company.

"Walt and Mary Ellen have a lot in common," Patrick said dryly, turning up the collar of his navy blue jacket for more protection from the icy wind. "They're *both* stubborn!"

"I think he was in love with her once," Olivia said quietly. "But he never did anything about it. And then I came along. . . ."

They walked along the lake in silence for a while before going home.

And the whole time, each was thinking of somebody else.

CHAPTER

Mary Ellen cornered Olivia in the locker room before practice on Monday. She gave Olivia the charge card, forcing herself to smile. Then she said casually, "Hey, Olivia, I heard the silliest thing. I heard you were out with Patrick Henley yesterday. Isn't that crazy?"

Olivia put the card in her gym bag and turned to Mary Ellen.

"No," she said, "it's not crazy at all," and watched Mary Ellen's face cave in. It serves her right for being such a snob, Olivia thought without sympathy. "I *was* with Patrick. He's a very nice person. But I guess you already know that."

"What about Walt?"

"In case you haven't noticed, Mary Ellen, Walt isn't speaking to me right now. C'mon, we'd better get going."

For a moment, Olivia did feel sorry for Mary Ellen, and was tempted to explain that she and

Patrick were just friends. But she decided against it. Maybe thinking she'd lost Patrick would make Mary Ellen see what she could have had all along.

Olivia picked up her pompons and headed for the gym. Mary Ellen followed silently.

On their way to the gym they ran into Pres, who snarled a greeting and stomped on ahead of them. The minute Kerry had called him the night before to tell him she was back from her grandparents', he had rushed right over to her house. But the loving reunion he'd expected was every bit as frustrating as all of their encounters had become.

"I'm sorry, Pres," she said, pulling away from him as she always did. "I'm sorry."

She was always sorry. Not as sorry as *he* was, though!

Most of the time he knew Kerry was right about the sex stuff. She was younger than he was, and he wouldn't feel right about pushing her into something. It would have been easier, he thought, if she was skinny and bony and maybe a little frigid. But Kerry was soft and warm and very, very loving.

And she was driving him crazy.

The evening with her had left him cranky and depressed, and he was totally unable to summon up any enthusiasm for this practice session.

Ardith Engborg had no way of knowing that Walt and Olivia were angry with each other, that Mary Ellen was frustrated by a lack of money and jealous of Patrick's sudden interest in Olivia, and that Pres was in a foul mood.

But by the time practice had ended, she had had it with all of them and she was more than ready to do something about it. She called them all together and told them to sit on the floor.

They know I'm going to read them the riot act, she thought, looking at six very attractive faces. And they know they've got it coming.

"The weekend after next," she said, "you will be spending partly with me. Your teamwork is practically nonexistent, your attitudes are poor, your timing is off, and while I don't know the details, I am well aware that some of you have allowed your personal problems to interfere with your work here."

She glanced at both Olivia and Walt as she made that statement. They flushed and stared at the floor.

"I simply will not allow dissension on the squad," she continued. "Not only does it create very sloppy teamwork, but it can be dangerous as well. Walt," she said sharply, "you nearly dropped Olivia just now doing that Around-the-World. You could have hurt her."

"I wasn't *trying* to," Walt mumbled.

Ardith looked startled. "Well, of course you weren't. I would never think such a thing!"

I would, Olivia thought. I would think such a thing.

"But you *were* careless," the coach added. "You're *all* becoming careless. And I won't have it."

"Now. What I have in mind is at least one full day of concentrated practice. Say, from seven in the morning till seven at night."

One loud, collective groan echoed throughout the gym.

She ignored it. "There will be exercises, tumbling, gymnastics, with the strongest concentration on teamwork. And I'm warning you all right now: If you don't bring the very best you have to offer, you may as well just stay home. Every single one of you can be immediately replaced."

The bleak looks that remark produced on six faces she was very fond of softened her somewhat, and she added, "But I'm sure I won't have to replace you. Whatever is wrong, this concentrated practice day should take care of it."

Olivia and Walt refrained from looking at each other. But they were both thinking the same thing: How could twelve straight hours of practice fix things between them? But they would attend. It was either that or quit the squad right now, and neither of them wanted that.

"I'm going to try to get the gym for that Saturday," Ardith said. "But if I can't there's a cabin out on the other side of the lake owned by a friend of mine, that might do. He's in Florida and if we have to borrow it for the day, I'm sure we'll be able to.

"In which case," she added, picking up her towel, "you'll need permission slips. I'll get them to you as soon as I know where we're going to be that day. In the meantime, we have a game tomorrow night." Fastening her eyes on them sternly, she added, "I expect you to perform as a team, not as a bunch of in-fighting, inexperienced juveniles!"

Meekly, they all promised they'd be ready to

lead Tarenton to victory against the Deep River Killers. They would be at their very best.

But they weren't.

In spite of Mary Ellen's resolve to leave her problems at home, she had a hard time giving her usual pre-game pep talk. Nothing she said sounded right, and it bothered her. She could tell from the way the others were behaving that they really needed that pep talk.

"The team needs us," she said in conclusion. "Deep River isn't an easy team to beat, you all know that. The guys need to know we're behind them all the way."

At first, she thought it had worked. The "Welcome" cheer went well and the crowd joined in enthusiastically. The pre-game cheering went smoothly and as they all ran off the floor just before the start of the game, things felt right to her. On her cheerleading roster for the evening, she had put Walt and Olivia together as little as possible, so she wasn't anticipating any major problems.

But her smugness didn't last long. The Deep River team was hot. Their defense, which in the past had always been weak, had strengthened since the last time Tarenton played them. It began to seem to Tarenton's Varsity Cheerleaders that every time Tarenton got the ball, a Deep River player managed to keep it out of the basket. The out-of-town team had always had a great offense, and the twos began adding up on the scoreboard under the word VISITORS.

Mary Ellen egged her squad on whenever

Deep River had the ball, yelling from the sidelines at the top of their lungs, "Steal it, steal it, take it away" and "We want the ball to go that-a-way, that-a-way," until they were nearly hoarse.

But she noticed during a Tarenton rush down the court with the ball that Olivia and Walt were much too quiet while the rest of the squad screamed "S-C-O-R-E" over and over.

At halftime, Ardith had a few choice words to say to her squad, especially Olivia and Walt.

"This is a game, not a funeral," she finished her lecture, looking directly at the two of them. "If you two don't put some enthusiasm into your movements and start thinking about your team instead of yourselves, I'm going to replace you. *Permanently!*"

She was really disgusted, and it showed. And they knew she meant what she said.

Mary Ellen watched their faces and was relieved to see new resolve there. She had no idea how they would act at the next practice session, but she was sure they would try harder tonight.

And they did.

Their halftime show, coming just seconds after Ardith's lecture, went smoothly, without a hitch. Olivia performed her routines flawlessly, her red and white skirt flying out around her, and the smile on her face seemed genuine. Walt, who always surprised the audience when his stocky body proved amazingly agile, never missed a step. Their finale, a perfectly executed jump-split, brought a roar of applause from both the home audience and the visitors.

They were always aware of a job well-done.

This time, it gave them the incentive they needed to do a better job during the second half.

Because Mary Ellen knew Ardith was keeping a keen eye on Olivia and Walt, and because she was sure now that they would do their best, she changed her roster to give them more to do.

When Troy Frederick was fouled, landing on the gym floor with a thud, Mary Ellen sent Olivia out to give him a rousing cheer. No lack of enthusiasm *there*. Olivia spun in the air like a top. And between quarters, Mary Ellen assigned an Around-the-World to Walt and Olivia — the same stunt they'd goofed up at practice. Olivia's slender body swung around Walt as if she weighed no more than a feather, and this time he looked as if he enjoyed holding her.

Ardith actually smiled, and Mary Ellen heaved a sigh of relief.

With such a bad start in the first half of the game, Tarenton might have lost. But Deep River had overextended itself, and by early in the fourth quarter the visiting team was showing definite signs of fatigue.

Taking advantage of that fact, Tarenton picked up its own spirits and went on to take the game 56 to 50. The hot, crowded gym erupted in cheers that shook the rafters.

"Well," Ardith Engborg said as the squad gathered up their megaphones and pompons, "that was better. But we're still going to take that long practice day."

High spirits at the success of both the squad and the team took the sting out of that announcement.

"Besides," Mary Ellen announced in the locker room, still feeling very good about the game and their cheering, "it might be fun. The forest primeval and all that. There's no way she'll be able to get the gym."

"Right!" Nancy said sarcastically. "Not to mention the fact that Pres will be out there in the wilderness without Kerry. And I will be there without Josh. So don't expect everyone to share your wild enthusiasm, okay?"

Mary Ellen made a face. She hadn't given a thought to Kerry's absence. She'd been too busy worrying about Olivia and Patrick.

Angie wondered aloud who would bring the food, while Olivia wondered silently if Walt would be speaking to her by then. He *had* seemed to thaw a little bit in the second half of tonight's game. Maybe. . . .

Later that week at practice, Ardith told them Mrs. Oetjen, the principal, had said there was no way they could heat the gym with the school closed.

"So it's off to the piney woods," she said, and got in return a more positive reaction than she had expected.

"If we have to practice a whole day," Angie said cheerfully, "we might as well make an adventure of it. Who's bringing the food?"

"I will," their coach said, "but don't expect junk food."

"We know, we know," Olivia teased, her spirits buoyed by the prospect of spending a whole day with Walt. "Our bodies are temples!"

Everyone laughed, including Walt. I was right,

Olivia thought happily, he *is* thawing a little.

Ardith said they would work out the details of practice day later, and handed each of them a permission slip. Which Olivia's mother refused to sign.

"You're not serious!" Olivia shouted. "You can't possibly be! I *have* to go!"

"You don't *have* to do any such thing," her mother responded calmly. She was sitting at the kitchen table dicing carrots into a bowl. "Mrs. Engborg has no business dragging you out there in the middle of winter. You said it was a summer cabin. There probably isn't even any heat. You'll all catch your death of —"

"Pneumonia," Olivia interrupted rudely. "I know. Mother, there's a wood stove and plenty of wood. Mrs. Engborg checked. She's a perfectly responsible person. You've let me go to all of the out-of-town games and nothing terrible has ever happened."

"That was different."

"*How* was it different?" Her mother was so stubborn. But Olivia was going to practice day if she had to tie and gag her mother and stick her in the hall closet for the day.

Her mother took the diced carrots to the sink to rinse them. "You went somewhere safe and warm on those trips," she said firmly. "Another high school. Nothing bad can happen to you at a high school."

She has obviously never heard of rivalry riots, Olivia thought.

"Out there in the woods," her mother continued relentlessly, "anything can happen. There are bears on that side of the lake, and rattle-snakes. And so far from everything . . . how does she expect an ambulance to get out there in time if there's an accident?"

Why does she always have to think in terms of disaster? Olivia thought hopelessly. "Mother," she tried, "we're not going hiking. We're not going camping. We're going to be *inside* the nice, warm, lovely cabin all day practicing. Mrs. Engborg is going to provide a lovely, nutritious lunch and we're not going to ask any bears or rattle-snakes to join us. Okay?"

Her mother turned to face her, wiping her hands on her apron. "No. Not okay. You are *not* going, and that's final."

Olivia stood up. Aware that she probably looked ridiculously small next to her mother, who was a large, big-boned woman, she fought the feeling of weakness and said, "Oh yes I am, Mother! I *am* going. And you can't stop me."

And she whirled around and stormed out of the kitchen and up to her room.

CHAPTER

M ary Ellen felt as if everything was closing in on her. She wasn't earning a cent toward her escape from Tarenton, her romantic life was a solid zero, and as if those two things weren't enough, she wasn't at all happy with the way things were going on the cheerleading squad.

The game against Wickfield the night before, for instance, had been a triumph for the team but a disaster for the squad.

She sat on her bed making a list of "Things To Take for Practice Day" and wrote BOOTS on the piece of paper. But the whole time, she was remembering with humiliation how foolish they had all looked the night before.

She had led the cheering with all her heart and soul, but the squad just wasn't with her. Lost in their own problems, they just hadn't been able to get involved in what they were supposed to be doing.

So she had stood out there on the floor, her

wheat-colored hair flying out around her face, her red and white skirt flashing, and led the whole school in one cheer after another, knowing the whole time that her squad wasn't behind her one hundred percent, the way they should have been.

> "One-two-three-four-five!
> We're the Wolves,
> We eat 'em alive!

> "One-two-three-four!
> We're huffin' and puffin'
> On Wickfield's door!"

She always knew they weren't with her when she could hear the sound of her own voice instead of one loud cheer in unison.

"I don't want to hear *me*," she had snapped at Olivia after a particularly weak

> "Catch us now,
> Here we come!
> We've got Wickfield
> On the run!"

"I want to hear *all* of us!"

As much as Mary Ellen loved cheerleading and being the center of attention on that gym floor in her beautiful red and white outfit, she knew perfectly well what they were there for — they were there to provide support for the team, and she couldn't do that all by herself.

Feeling alone knocked off her own sense of timing, her cheeks flamed as she remembered staggering at the conclusion of a straddle jump. The false movement had been slight, but noticeable, and she'd been mortified.

The pep talk Ardith gave them during halftime hadn't helped — not that Mary Ellen could see, anyway. Pres, a perfectionist at cartwheels, actually lost his balance twice: Once he fell against Nancy, who gave him a dirty look in response; the second time he recovered by himself.

After faltering in the first half, the Tarenton Wolves picked up speed in the second half and, thanks to a lot of fouling on Wickfield's part, pulled ahead by two baskets.

The tension caused by such a tight score finally invigorated the Varsity Cheerleaders, Mary Ellen reflected as she wrote SCARF and GLOVES on her list. During the last fifteen minutes of the game, they had finally put some enthusiasm into their routines. And when they ran out onto the floor to yell

"Go! Go! Go!
We're with you,
Go! Go! Go!
See it through,
Keep it goin',
Keep it flowin',
Yeah, team, yeah, team, yeah, team!"

Mary Ellen had definitely heard six voices, not just her own.

But as far as she was concerned, it was too late. They had all looked like amateurs out there, with the whole school watching.

91

Tarenton won by a mere two points. No thanks to us, Mary Ellen thought bitterly. It's a good thing Ardith had already scheduled practice day, or we'd really be in hot water now!

She sat on her bed, pencil in hand, wondering if there would be any point in trying to catch Pres alone on practice day.

Probably not, she thought. True, she and Pres had dated some in the past. But then, there were few girls at Tarenton High who hadn't gone out with the handsome, rich Preston Tilford III. Until Kerry Elliot came along.

Mary Ellen had never expected Pres to fall so hard for anyone, least of all Kerry, who wasn't that gorgeous. A little too plump, for one thing. She'd never be a model. But then, she probably didn't want to be one. She seemed perfectly content to just be Pres's girl. Even though, Mary Ellen thought emphatically, they have absolutely nothing in common!

Kerry Elliot was at that moment thinking exactly the same thing. She was sitting in the front seat of Pres's Porsche, parked in the Elliots' driveway, and she was crying.

Pres put his arm around the back of Kerry's bucket seat and leaned closer to her. "Look," he said earnestly, "all I said was, what Olivia did at Walt's party wasn't such a big deal. She'd had too much to drink and she didn't know what she was doing. What does it have to do with us, anyway?"

"I knew you'd defend Olivia," Kerry said, sniffing. "You think I'm being silly. I just know how *I'd* feel if I found *you* with somebody else, making out."

He really didn't feel like dealing with this right now. He was still smarting from his mistakes on the floor at the Wickfield game, his father had been on his back again about going into the family business, and school was a drag. He had counted on Kerry to cheer him up. Instead, here she was giving him a hard time. Not only had she pushed him away as she always did just when they were really getting going, but now she'd had to go and bring up this stupid business with Walt and Olivia.

"I'm *not* Olivia," he said, annoyed, "and I didn't say what she did was okay. I just said she didn't know what she was doing. Okay?"

"No, it's not okay," Kerry said, surprising him. "I know you wish I was more sophisticated, like Vanessa and Mary Ellen. I feel it more and more all the time."

"That's not true!" he shouted.

"Yes, it *is*! I know you're frustrated because I'm . . . because I won't go to bed with you. You hardly ever say anything about it, and I'm grateful for that. But you're so tense all the time, and I feel like it's my fault."

"Kerry," he began, "I understand —" but she interrupted him.

"I'm just afraid you're going to go looking for somebody else. Someone like Vanessa. Well, I wish I *was* more like Vanessa, but I'm not. And I can't be."

"I don't want you to be."

"I think you do. At least part of you. The part that defends Olivia when she hurt Walt so badly. That really makes me wonder, Pres. It makes me wonder if you wouldn't do the same thing."

And as he watched in shocked silence, she opened the car door and got out. Before she closed the door, she said with tears in her voice, "I want to trust you, Pres. I really do. But it's hard. And I know you'd be better off with somebody who doesn't give you such a hard time . . . someone more your type."

And she was gone, across the lawn and up the steps into her house.

The porch light went out.

He couldn't believe any of this had happened. He sat there, stunned. Why was she doing this? Because of Olivia? And Walt? That was crazy!

It was all his fault. He'd made too much of his frustration when they kissed good-night. All that heavy sighing! Now Kerry was convinced he was looking for casual sex, just the way she thought Olivia had.

He was tired of girls like Vanessa, girls who knew all the right moves. Kerry was different. But now that very difference was causing him trouble.

So what did she want from him — a guarantee? He'd told her he wouldn't do what Olivia had done, and she'd chosen not to believe him. Wasn't that *her* problem?

Pres Tilford didn't give guarantees. She might as well find that out right now. She'd call him. She would. When she'd had time to realize how silly she'd been, she'd go straight to the phone.

Wouldn't she?

He roared out of the driveway and headed home.

CHAPTER

Olivia didn't know what to do about her permission slip. Ardith was getting impatient and Olivia's mother wouldn't budge. Every time Olivia brought up the subject, her mother sniffed and made some comment about Mrs. Engborg needing "her head examined." Most of these discussions took place at the dinner table and Olivia's father suffered through them silently.

But just when Olivia was beginning to think seriously of forging her mother's signature, her father appeared in the doorway to her room, knocking gently on the frame.

"May I come in?" In place of his usual gray suit, crisp white shirt, and dark tie, he was wearing tan pants and a navy blue sweater. Her father never wore jeans.

"Sure, Dad. Come on in."

Being in the same room alone with him was awkward. She never talked to her father for more than a minute or two: "Good morning," "Good evening," and "Did you have a nice day?" — that sort of thing. It was almost as though her parents had an unwritten agreement that her father would handle the bills while her mother handled Olivia.

"Could I see that permission slip you and your mother were talking about?" he asked.

"Sure." She wondered what he wanted it for. He wasn't going to tear it up, was he? She handed it to him. He stood in the middle of her room, reading it.

Then he looked up. "Got a pen?" The eyes behind his horn-rimmed glasses were sympathetic.

She handed him a pen. "Daddy" — how long since she had called him that? — "Mom will kill you."

"I'll handle your mother. You said this was important, right?"

She nodded.

"Okay, then." And he signed the form, ending with a dramatic flourish. "There you go," he said, handing pen and paper back to her.

She threw her arms around him and gave him a big hug. "Thanks, Daddy. Thanks a lot! I just hope you're not sorry you did this."

"Um-hum," he said absentmindedly, patting her hair. "You're a good girl, Olivia."

After he'd left, Olivia danced around the room, clutching the precious piece of paper in her hand. A whole day with Walt! If she couldn't win him back out at the lake. . . . But I *will* get him back, she resolved. I *will*!

Mary Ellen, feeling sisterly, took Gemma with

her when she went to the mall to buy new boots.

After half an hour or so of pricing, they were both depressed.

"I am so tired of always looking at the price tag first," Mary Ellen said in disgust as they came out of their fifth shoe store empty-handed.

She hadn't intended to go anywhere near Marnie's. Too depressing, and she certainly didn't need that now. But she wasn't paying attention to where they were going and suddenly, there was Vanessa, posed on the little platform in front of the store, looking disgustingly gorgeous in a beautiful royal blue sweater dress and blue suede boots.

"Hi, there, Mary Ellen," she said, looking down at the two sisters.

"Are you allowed to talk?" Mary Ellen asked acidly.

Vanessa shrugged. "She can't see me. She's with a customer, anyway."

Another shrug. "You have no idea how painfully boring this is! Anyone who wants to model for a living is just plain stupid!"

Mary Ellen grinned, feeling a surge of hope. Vanessa did look very impressive up there on that platform, she couldn't deny that. People walking by in the mall practically bumped heads craning their necks to get a good look at her. The tall, dark-haired, very exotic Vanessa made a good model. But if she disobeyed orders regularly, and if she was bored. . . .

Maybe she'll get fired. Or quit.

If she quits, Mary Ellen thought as she spotted Angie and her brother Andrew coming toward them, maybe I can talk Mrs. Gunderson into letting me take her place two afternoons a week.

"By the way," Vanessa called sweetly as Mary Ellen turned away, "Olivia and Patrick just went by. Did you see them?"

Mary Ellen's spirits, momentarily lifted by the faint hope of possible employment, slid back down into her old boots with a thud. She still hadn't admitted that Patrick and Olivia might have something going. But if I see them together, she thought unhappily, I might have to admit it.

Angie and Andrew called to them, and came over.

"Vanessa looks bored to tears," Angie commented, bringing forth a more enthusiastic greeting than usual from Mary Ellen. "You shopping?"

"Boots. I need new boots."

"Great! So do I. There's a new discount place right around the corner. We can check it out together."

Well, if any of Mary Ellen's fellow cheerleaders had to see how little money she had to spend, she'd prefer that it was Angie. Angie didn't have much money, either.

"Okay, why not? Let's go and leave Vanessa to her admirers."

Angie and Mary Ellen found a display of warm, good-looking boots on sale at the new shoe store, and were still congratulating themselves for clever shopping when they left the store, Andrew and Gemma trailing along behind.

They turned a corner, laughing, and came face-to-face with Olivia and Patrick.

Mary Ellen's heart felt as if it were tissue

paper being ripped from a gift, and wondered miserably if the sight of Patrick was always going to do something to her insides — if she would always have this wild urge to walk over to him and lay her head on his chest, forgetting everything in the world except how wonderful he felt.

Angie hadn't yet heard any rumors about Olivia and Patrick, and simply said, "Hi, guys. What's going on?"

Mary Ellen and Patrick looked at each other. She looked away first.

Olivia cleared her throat and said, "My dad signed my permission slip, so I decided it was safe to go out and get new boots. Patrick said he'd help me."

"How sweet of him," Mary Ellen murmured, glancing down at the huge package Patrick was carrying under his arm. The bag read SLOANE'S, of course. No discount shoe store for Olivia Evans!

"That's me," Patrick said, grinning down at Mary Ellen, "sweet to the very core."

He knows I'm jealous, she thought, furious. And he loves it!

"Why don't we all get something to drink," Angie suggested, "since we all got what we came for. We'll celebrate."

The last thing in the world Mary Ellen felt like doing was celebrating. "I can't," she said sharply, avoiding Patrick's eyes. "We've got to get home. You guys go ahead, though."

And she grabbed Gemma's hand and dragged her away.

During the ride home, her body may have been on the noisy, overcrowded bus, but her heart was back at the mall with Patrick. She sighed and stared out the bus window until they reached their stop.

Kerry Elliot, alone in her bedroom, wiped her eyes and thought about how being a Varsity Cheerleader's girl friend had changed her life. All the attention, all the excitement — it was fun. And Pres was fun and interesting and popular, and was gentle and loving. Most of the time.

She didn't want to lose all of that. She didn't want to lose Pres. But how could she trust him?

Her mother had said, "He's a nice enough boy. But he's much too sophisticated for you."

She means I'm not like Vanessa or Mary Ellen, Kerry thought as she lay on her bed, surrounded by crumpled tissues, her eyes swollen and red. She thinks Pres wants someone like Vanessa, too.

I shouldn't have made such a big deal out of that business with Olivia. It's not as though Pres has been pressuring me much about sex. He hasn't. But I know he thinks about it all the time.

I wonder if he knows *I* think about it all the time, too. I might not be ready for it, even with Pres, but that doesn't stop me from thinking about it.

Why doesn't he call and try to make up? She started crying again.

At that very moment, Pres was standing where, only moments before, Mary Ellen and Gemma had been standing. He was watching Vanessa Barlow turn heads. And he was thinking how easy it would be to offer her a ride home in his

Porsche. She'd jump at the chance. She always did. They could drive out to Lookout Point. . . .

Vanessa threw him a megawatt smile that jolted his entire body. It probably wouldn't have worked if Pres and Kerry hadn't had their argument, but they had.

"Want a ride home?" he called to Vanessa, and she lit up like a Christmas tree.

"You bet!" she mouthed. "Out back in fifteen minutes!"

He ran into Olivia and Patrick, Angie and Andrew while he was waiting for Vanessa. They wanted to know what he was doing, and he told them. Why not? Olivia raised her eyebrows, but nobody said anything.

Pres thought Andrew looked a little hopeful, though. He was probably still crazy about Kerry, even though she'd gone from him to Pres.

How had things gotten so crazy? he wondered, watching them walk away. What was Olivia doing with Patrick? She was supposed to be with Walt. And why was he waiting for Vanessa? He didn't even *like* Vanessa that much. She was a champion troublemaker.

But she likes *me*, he thought, and that's what I want right now. I want to be with somebody who likes me and isn't giving me ultimatums.

They drove out to Lookout Point. Vanessa chattered all the way there, tossing her long black hair and saying how much she'd missed him.

He parked the car and reached for her. She responded eagerly when he began kissing her, and that felt good to him. *She* didn't care what

101

he thought about Olivia's behavior at Walt's party. In fact, she probably felt pretty much the same as he did about it, unlike Kerry, who disapproved.

Vanessa wound her arms around his neck and murmured his name. She felt warm and soft and he knew he could lose himself in her if he really wanted to. He could forget all of his petty little problems and make both himself and Vanessa happy.

But something was wrong, because he really didn't want to do this. Well, he *did* and he *didn't*. The feelings Vanessa aroused in him were strong. His body was saying, "Sure, why not?"

But something inside him was warning, "If you keep kissing Vanessa, you're kissing Kerry goodbye."

Kerry had said he would be better off with someone his "own type." He didn't want Vanessa to be his type. He didn't want Kerry to be right. Not this time. He pulled away from Vanessa's lips and arms so fast, she must have thought he was having a seizure.

"What are you doing?" she cried as he turned the ignition key and turned the Porsche toward town.

"Sorry," he mumbled, feeling like the worst fool in the world. "I just remembered I have a really important appointment."

She ranted and raved at him all the way back to town.

When she left the Porsche, she said coldly, "Thanks for nothing. I feel sorry for your cute little girl friend. She's dealing with a crazy!"

Then she slammed the door and was gone.

He thought about going straight to Kerry's house. But he couldn't. Someone had probably already told her he'd been seen waiting for Vanessa. Andrew, probably.

If Andrew had, Kerry would never believe him when he told her nothing had happened. Well . . . almost nothing. Why *should* she believe him? He'd done exactly what she'd been worried about in the first place.

The darkness he drove through on his way home matched his mood.

CHAPTER

Kerry had decided she'd behaved badly. She'd had no real reason to mistrust Pres. She was on her way to find him and apologize, skipping her study hall, when she ran into Vanessa in the hall.

Kerry had worn her best plaid skirt and rust blouse and had brushed her hair until it shone, but standing next to Vanessa, elegant in velvet designer jeans and a cream-colored silk shirt, she felt like a toad.

I will never look like that, she thought with certainty, not in a zillion years. Not even if I starve off twenty pounds and have plastic surgery.

What was it like to look like Vanessa?

Aloud, she asked the girl who had stopped her in the hall, "What do you want, Vanessa?"

Vanessa smiled. "I just wanted to know if you'd seen Pres," she said in a silky voice. "Or if you'd be seeing him today. I think I left my library card in his car."

Kerry almost laughed out loud. Vanessa at the library would be like a vegetarian attending a barbecue.

"Or maybe," Vanessa added, smiling beautifully, "it fell out at Lookout Point."

Vanessa and Pres? At Lookout Point?

Well, hadn't she told him to find somebody else more his type? Yes, but he didn't have to do it, did he? So quickly?

Kerry mumbled something and walked away, her senses numbed. She'd been looking for Pres to apologize, hadn't she? Boy, what a jerk I am, she thought angrily. He goes running off to comfort himself with Vanessa while I'm crying my eyes out, and *I'm* the one who's ready to apologize.

By noon, it was all over school that Pres had taken Vanessa to Lookout Point. Kerry walked into the cafeteria with her head held high, determined not to admit to anyone that she was dying inside. When Pres appeared at the table she was sharing with Nancy and Josh, he had to say her name twice before she would even look at him.

"C'mon outside," he said. "I need to talk to you. Please!"

If she got up and followed him, everyone in the cafeteria would stare at them. Everyone would point and whisper. She'd hate that. But if she didn't go with him, he'd make a scene. She'd hate that, too.

She got up and followed him out of the cafeteria. He led the way to a small alcove under the stairs. They faced each other, but before he

105

could open his mouth, she said coolly, "I was looking for you so I could apologize, but I ran into Vanessa first."

"Vanessa?" he said uneasily. "Haven't you learned by now that Vanessa's main mission in life is to make trouble? Why do you listen to her?"

"Pres, did you take her to Lookout Point?"

"I took her there," he admitted, avoiding her eyes. "I was mad at you, so I acted like a kid and went straight for Vanessa."

Kerry watched his face. She said nothing, but her eyes were very bright.

"But I changed my mind," he said, still not looking at her. "I didn't want to be with her. I wanted to be with you."

A very clear vision of Pres and Vanessa wrapped around each other in the Porsche clouded Kerry's vision. She passed a hand across her eyes and looked up at Pres.

"I'm glad you changed your mind," she said slowly. "I really want to believe you're telling me the truth about that. Because I *need* to. I'm not like your other friends. I can't laugh off things like Olivia and Walt at his party, and you and Vanessa fooling around at Lookout Point. I wish I could, but I can't."

"I don't want you to."

"Yes, you *do*. You want me to be more casual about things like that. But Pres," and her eyes fixed on his, "if I were, maybe I'd be more casual about us, too. Did you ever think of that? And maybe I'd do what Olivia did."

He couldn't imagine that.

Reading his thoughts, she nodded. "You're so sure I wouldn't do that, aren't you? And that feels good, doesn't it? Well, I'm entitled to the same thing from you. I have a right to be sure you wouldn't do something like that anymore than I would. I *need* that from you, Pres."

Her round face was very pale. "And until you're willing to give me that, I don't think we should see each other." She turned away from him and hurried off down the hall.

Pres watched her go, frowning. He'd blown it this time, for sure. Kerry had always been so easy to get along with. He'd always been able to handle her. How could he have known she'd suddenly starting giving orders and ultimatums? As if she owned him? Well, she didn't own him. Nobody did. He was still his own person.

Hands in his pockets, head down, he went to his government class. But he had trouble concentrating. He was simply unable to accept the fact that he, of all people, was having woman problems. He just didn't understand anything any more.

In the cafeteria, Nancy was busy filling Josh in on the latest gossip about Pres and Vanessa. He listened politely, his dark eyes fixed on her, his broad face serious. When she had finished with a disgusted, "Honestly, Pres acts like such a baby sometimes!" Josh nodded his dark head in agreement.

"Yeah. Well. Hey, want to come over and listen to some records tonight? We can work on our term papers together."

"And Walt and Olivia are really messing up

lately, too," Nancy said, as if Josh hadn't spoken. "That game at Wickfield. . . ." She shuddered. "It was a disaster. Well, you saw it. I tried talking to Olivia, but she just brushed me off. I don't think that girl even *wants* any help. She doesn't seem to care that their stupid romantic problems are affecting the whole squad."

Josh stood up. "Listen, I've gotta go," he said abruptly, picking up his books. "See you later."

Nancy stared in surprise, her mouth open, as he left her sitting there alone. What on earth was going on? Why had he left without her? They always walked to class together. Maybe he wasn't feeling well. But he hadn't said anything about being sick. They were supposed to go for pizza after school. And hadn't he said something about the two of them studying together later?

She left the cafeteria alone, but she wasn't thinking about Josh along the way. She was brooding about the problems on the squad.

Since there was no practice scheduled after school, Mary Ellen headed for the mall. She had no money, but Vanessa had been complaining in gym class about her job at Marnie's. Maybe she was ready to quit, and if she was, Mary Ellen wanted to make sure Mrs. Gunderson knew she was still interested in the job.

Marnie's owner said she would keep her in mind, even though Mary Ellen had to admit that she still had only two afternoons a week free.

Judging from the expression on Vanessa's face as Mary Ellen passed her outside the store,

Mrs. Gunderson just might *need* a new model soon. Vanessa looked bored silly.

When she passed Pizza Corner, she saw Nancy and Josh sitting in a corner with Walt, and thought about joining them. She decided against it. Being around Walt these days was like spending time in a funeral parlor. Going home and studying would be festive compared to sitting with Walt.

Studying was exactly what Walt was discussing with Nancy and Josh, in a tone of voice usually reserved for news announcers reporting a plane crash with no survivors.

"I can't think," he told them morosely, his head in his hands. "I can't concentrate."

"But your grades have been okay, haven't they?" Nancy asked. "I thought you were doing better this year."

"That was *Olivia!*" Walt cried, lifting his head and looking at her with mournful eyes. "She studied with me. She helped me understand some of the stuff and it was easier and more fun with her. She made me *feel* like studying. Now it just doesn't seem important."

Josh and Nancy listened sympathetically, while their pizza lay untouched on the table, getting colder by the minute.

"Listen, Walt," Nancy said earnestly, "I think you should call Olivia."

"Are you kidding? She isn't speaking to me. How can I call her?"

"Simple. Just pick up the phone and dial her number. She thinks you're still upset about your party."

Walt flushed.

"I know how sorry she is about that night," Nancy added hastily, brushing her long dark brown hair away from her face. "I heard her telling someone how awful she felt about the whole thing."

Walt looked at her suspiciously. "Really?"

"Honest." Well, so it was a little white lie. She couldn't actually remember hearing those specific words from Olivia, but she could tell by the way the girl acted when Walt was around that she *was* sorry.

Walt looked doubtful. And he wasn't eating, which Nancy saw as a definite sign that he really was miserable.

"Call Olivia," she urged softly. "Call her! It can't hurt, and it will probably help. Go home and do it. Now!"

Shaking his head, he left. When he had gone, Josh asked Nancy if she'd like to go to a concert Saturday night.

"I wonder if he'll actually call her," she mused, picking up a slice of pizza. "It would certainly make a big difference on the squad if they made up." Then she looked at him. "Did you say something?"

Josh shook his head. He didn't repeat the concert invitation.

Nancy didn't even notice that he was unusually quiet during the ride to her house, or that his good-bye kiss was just a peck on the cheek. She was lost in her own thoughts.

It took Walt a while to work up the courage to phone Olivia. First he combed his hair three times, clipped his fingernails a little too savagely, and did some stretching exercises. The exercises did the trick. With his stomach doing jump shots, he went to the telephone in the den and dialed Olivia's number. Then he stopped breathing.

She answered the phone with a cheerful, "Hello?"

He breathed again. "Olivia? It's Walt."

Silence. Then, an uncertain, "Oh. Hi, Walt." Nothing more.

She wasn't going to help him out at all. She could have added something like, "Anything wrong?" and then he could have told her how much trouble he was having studying. But she hadn't.

He was going to have to do it all himself. "Olivia," he began, keeping his voice as smooth as possible, "I was wondering. . . . Well, I was just wondering if you were doing anything tonight." Before she could say, Yes, I am, or, No, I'm not, he hurried on. "I mean, I'd really like to talk to you. If you feel like it. If you're not busy."

He was so flustered by this time, he ran a hand through his hair, making it stand up all over his head. His stomach was churning like the Jeep wheels stuck in a snowdrift.

"I'd love to see you, Walt," she said, and her voice was so warm it soothed his stomach and eased his breathing problems. Until she added, "But I can't. I'm sorry."

He wasn't ready to give up. It had taken too much just to make this phone call.

"Well, if you have to go somewhere," he offered, "maybe I could take you there and wait

111

for you, and then we could go get something to eat afterwards."

Was he begging? It sounded like begging to him. If she said no, he would despise himself forever.

She said no. She said it nicely, her voice apologetic, but it was still no.

"I already have a ride," was the response that made Walt's toes curl in shame. "I'm sorry. I really am."

She was going out with Patrick. He was sure of it.

"Walt? Are you still there? Listen, couldn't we make it tomorrow night?"

Walt found rejection totally humiliating, no matter how nicely it was phrased. Taking the initiative with a girl was a gamble every time. The girl could be nice about saying no, and he'd still feel stupid. Or the girl could be rude and act as if he'd lost his mind thinking someone as wonderful as she would even think about going out with a jerk like him, and he'd hang up the phone feeling stupid and foolish and worthless.

Or the girl could be someone he loved a lot and thought he was safe with, and she could shoot him down just like the others.

He hated it. He had always hated it. And it had always made him angry, the unfairness of it.

It made him angry now. He had swallowed his pride and called Olivia, even though everything had been *her* fault, not his. And look what had happened — more humiliation.

Who needed it? Patrick could have her. He'd

heard all about *that*. And the next time he saw Nancy. . . .

"Gee, I can't make it tomorrow night," he said in mock apology. "Sorry."

"Walt —" she began.

He hung up.

Afterwards, he was never sure exactly why he headed for his parents' liquor cabinet. Walt wasn't a drinker. He'd had sips of hard liquor at his parents' parties and in his own private opinion the stuff tasted like something you'd pour into a car's engine.

But he felt as if he had to do *something* or he'd explode. He didn't want to call anyone, and he didn't want to go out, and he wasn't hungry. His parents weren't home, and even if they had been, he wouldn't have talked to them about this. How do you tell Mr. and Mrs. Small-Town Popularity that their only son has been striking out in practically every area of his life?

It never once occurred to Walt that Olivia hadn't actually said she was going out with Patrick. Shaking his head, he walked over to the bar, picked up a decanter, and sloshed several inches of brownish liquid into a glass. Then he took the glass and went over to sit on the window seat overlooking the patio.

CHAPTER

13

Olivia replaced the receiver after talking to Walt, and turned to face a very angry mother.

"I can't believe you're turning down that nice Walt Manners for that Henley boy!" Mrs. Evans said in disgust. Her cheeks were as red as her cardigan sweater.

"What you really mean, Mother," Olivia replied coldly, "is that you can't believe I'm turning down the son of celebrities to go out with a garbage collector."

"Olivia," her mother begged, "think what you're doing. You know it's Walt you really care about. You're acting like a child, trying to make him jealous."

"For your information, I'm not doing any such thing! I'm not even seeing Patrick tonight, and I never told Walt that I was. I'm going shopping with Shelley Eismar. Walt never gave me a chance to tell him that.

"Besides," she pointed out as she turned to

leave the kitchen, "haven't you always told me never to accept last-minute invitations? You said," she added with a wicked grin, "that the boys would think I was too anxious!"

When Walt's parents arrived home, they found him wandering around on the patio. Although the air was frigid, Walt's feet were bare and he was wearing only a plaid flannel shirt and jeans. He was singing the Tarenton Fight Song, waving an empty glass in the air as he sang. His round face was flushed, and it was obvious to his parents that he wasn't feeling the cold.

When his father got close enough to take Walt's arm and lead him into the house, he understood with one quick whiff of Walt's breath why Walt was feeling no pain.

Closing the patio door and taking the bar glass from Walt, Mr. Manners asked, "How many of these have you had?"

Walt grinned dopily. "Six hundred and seventy-three," he said, and laughed hilariously before falling, face first, onto the couch, where he lay as still as if he'd been felled by an axe.

"He ever get into the liquor before?" his father asked Walt's mother.

She shook her head. "Not that I know of." She covered her son with an afghan and stood looking down at him, sympathy in her face. "I think he's having problems with Olivia. She hasn't been over here in a while, and he seems depressed."

"Well, drinking himself silly isn't going to get his girl back," he said matter-of-factly. He shook his head. "He makes a lousy drunk. I hope he's learned his lesson."

They turned off the light and went to bed, prepared to lecture Walt in the morning when his head was clear. But Walt remembered absolutely nothing the following morning.

"On the patio? In my bare feet? What are you guys talking about?" Then, because he knew they would never invent such a story, he asked slowly, "Did I *really* do all that? How come I don't remember it?"

They gave him a mild lecture on the hazards of abusing alcohol and let him go to school.

Driving there, Walt tried to sort things out. Not remembering made him feel as if his life had belonged to somebody else the night before. He'd had no control over what he'd done. The liquor had been in charge. He was beginning to understand how little control Olivia must have had over *her* actions on the night of his party. And he was beginning to feel very guilty about the way he'd treated her. Hadn't she said, "Walt, I didn't know what I was doing"? And he hadn't believed her.

Well, he believed her now. But it was probably too late.

Parking the Jeep in the school lot, he got out and headed for the entrance. His mouth dropped open as he spotted the huge red and white banner draped over the big wooden doors.

It read: GO TARENTON! GOUGE GARRISON!

They had a game in Garrison tonight. He'd completely forgotten about it. What was happening to his brain, anyway? It was a wonder he remembered his own name!

116

An "away" game. His spirits lifted. He and Olivia always sat together for away games. Always. It was . . . understood.

This would be their first away game since their fight. Would she sit with him? If she did, they could talk. He could tell her how stupid he'd been. He could even tell her about last night. They'd have a good laugh about it. He could tell her he was sorry. He *needed* to tell Olivia that he was sorry.

Patrick Henley wouldn't be on the bus. He wasn't a cheerleader. So there wouldn't be any reason for Olivia *not* to sit with Walt. Who else would she sit with?

She sat with Pres.

Walt couldn't believe his eyes when he climbed into the bus and saw her sitting there in a front seat, next to the window, with Pres sitting where Walt should have been — beside Olivia.

He was bitterly disappointed. He'd been looking forward to this bus ride all day. He'd even hoped maybe she was looking forward to it, too. What was she doing sitting with Pres?

As Walt walked back to take an empty seat behind Mary Ellen and Angie, his face tight with anger, Olivia was trying hard not to burst into tears.

She *had* been looking forward to this chance to sit with Walt. She missed him terribly. Patrick was nice, but he wasn't Walt. She'd counted on tonight to make things right between them. What was the matter with Pres, anyway? He *knew* she always sat with Walt on these trips. Biting her lip, she ignored Pres and stared out the window.

Pres had taken the empty seat beside Olivia because he was sure Walt wouldn't. That would embarrass Olivia and humiliate her, and a humiliated cheerleader is not a good cheerleader. It would throw off her timing. And one person's bad timing can ruin an entire squad's efforts; Pres knew that. They would all look like fools at Garrison. Pres was not at all keen on looking like a fool. So he took Walt's seat.

They were not a happy group as the bus pulled away from Tarenton High School on its way to Garrison.

Nancy missed Josh terribly. She wished he was still on the squad. She was worried about him, too. He just didn't seem himself lately. She couldn't put her finger on what was wrong. He'd been so quiet. And he hadn't come over last night. Hadn't even phoned. When she'd called his house, his mother said he was sleeping. Sleeping? She was beginning to wonder if he had his eye on another girl.

By the time they boarded the bus after the game, Pres had to admit that sitting with Olivia hadn't done any good at all. They had looked like fools, anyway. The whole game had been one mistake after another for Tarenton's Varsity Cheerleaders. Lousy timing, no concentration, lack of enthusiasm, you name it, he thought bitterly — we had it all!

Mary Ellen stared out the window, wondering if Ardith would replace them the very next day. It would serve us right if she does, she thought miserably, remembering the triumphant look on Vanessa Barlow's face when Walt bumped into

Olivia during a series of cartwheels and sent her flying. Mary Ellen had always suspected that the only reason Vanessa got to every game early enough to get a seat in front was so she could keep an eye on any mistakes the cheerleaders might make. Heaven knows she'd had plenty of material to crow about tonight!

Mary Ellen sent a nasty look across the aisle toward Olivia. It was all her fault. Her and her stupid problems with Walt. When was it going to end?

Olivia was so lost in her own misery, she didn't see Mary Ellen's look of disgust. She sat beside Pres, slumped down in her seat, seeing over and over again the horrid fall she'd taken when Walt had smacked into her. Her cheeks flamed and her eyes closed in humiliation.

"Boy, we were sure lousy tonight!" Pres said, echoing Mary Ellen's thoughts as the bus got underway.

Mary Ellen made a sound of disgust and said in a loud voice, "You can say that again! And say it loud enough for Walt and Olivia to hear!"

Olivia knew Mary Ellen was right. But hearing it said aloud like that in front of the other cheerleaders and the basketball team made her defensive. "Well, the team won, didn't they?"

"Yeah, no thanks to us," Mary Ellen replied.

"Well, it's the *captain's* responsibility to make the squad work!" Olivia accused. "And I guess you didn't do such a hot job of that tonight, did you?"

Angie, playing peacemaker as usual, said, "Olivia's not the only one who goofed tonight.

We all made mistakes. Our timing was off."

"*My* timing wasn't off!" Nancy snapped, giving Angie a disgusted look. "But Pres almost killed me during the 'Hello' cheer. He wasn't paying the slightest bit of attention to what he was doing."

"Well, *excuse* me!" Pres said, swiveling his head to give Nancy an indignant look. "I didn't notice a whole lot of concentration on your part, either. Thinking about your absent boyfriend, I suppose. I noticed he wasn't at the game tonight."

"At least I've only got *one* boyfriend," Nancy pointed out heatedly. "No wonder you can't pay attention to anything as trivial as cheerleading. You're so busy balancing girls you can't see straight!"

"Leave my love life out of this!"

"All *right*! That's enough!" Ardith shouted, standing up in the aisle. "This is not the time or the place. And I've had just about enough out of all of you. Not another word! We will hash this out later."

They quieted down then and while Angie and Ardith dozed, the others sulked silently, while in the back of the bus the team celebrated their victory, joking, and singing fight songs. None of the cheerleaders joined in.

When they arrived at school, Josh was waiting for Nancy. She hadn't expected him to meet her, since he hadn't been at the game, and she was delighted to see him. Josh was just what she needed. Without telling anyone good-night, she ran over and kissed him, then climbed into his car.

And Patrick was there, standing beside his truck. Mary Ellen spotted him and thought, he must be waiting for Olivia. Oh, great, this just makes my day!

Olivia saw him and thought exactly the same thing. It never occurred to her that Patrick might be waiting for somebody else.

But in fact, he had been waiting for Mary Ellen. He hoped that if she saw him standing there alone, she'd come over to say hello. Then he could offer to take her home. He fully expected Olivia to ride with Walt. She had told Patrick that she intended to patch things up with him during the ride to Garrison. So he was surprised when Olivia climbed down from the bus, saw him standing there, and headed straight for him.

He looked over at Mary Ellen and their eyes met. He tried to send her a mental message that said, I'd really rather be with you. That's why I'm here. But you can understand that I can't just tell Olivia to get lost, can't you?

He couldn't tell whether or not she got his message. She turned away just as Olivia said, "Hi, Patrick, I'm so glad you're here!"

Walt watched Olivia go to Patrick and felt totally defeated. So she didn't want to sit with him on the bus and she didn't want to ride home with him. Okay. He didn't have to be hit on the head with a brick. The realization that he had never bothered to *ask* Olivia to ride home with him escaped him. He drove home alone, feeling very sorry for himself.

Josh listened patiently to Nancy's tirade about

the failings of the Tarenton Varsity Cheerleading Squad all the way to her house. But when he had switched off the ignition, he turned to her and said quietly, "Nancy, I don't want to hear one more word about cheerleading. You got that?"

She stared at him.

"I have had it with that squad!" he continued. "Don't you ever think of anything else?"

"Josh —"

"Look," he said, "I know it's important to you. But I thought *I* was important to you, too."

"You *are!*"

"Yeah, right. Half the time you don't even hear me when I'm talking to you. Your head is with that squad twenty-four hours a day."

"You just don't understand what a mess everything is!" she shouted angrily. "Don't you *care* that it's making me miserable?"

"I care. You're the one who doesn't care — about anything except that squad. Where does that leave me?"

Before she could say anything, he shook his head and said, "C'mon, let's go. I'm tired."

And he was out of the car, slamming the door after him.

What was wrong with Josh was finally beginning to sink into Nancy's mind. It frightened her. She'd never seen him so angry. Were they going to end up like Olivia and Walt?

Josh yanked her door open. "C'mon!" he said impatiently, looking over her head.

He wasn't acting like himself at all. It was all her fault, Nancy knew that. He was right. About everything. No wonder he'd been so quiet lately.

She'd been in some kind of fog over problems on the squad, and she'd left him out in the cold.

They walked to her front door in silence. She felt cold all over, and she knew it wasn't just the night air. She wasn't sure how to begin patching things up. Maybe it was too late. Maybe she'd been ignoring him too long and he wouldn't listen to her now. But she had to try.

"Josh," she said hesitantly as she turned to face him, "I'm . . . I'm sorry. Honest." She put her arms around his waist and looked directly into his eyes. "You're right about everything, and I promise it won't happen again. I won't shut you out again."

He looked at her silently and his body felt stiff and unyielding.

Let me do this right, she prayed. "You're more important to me than the squad," she said softly. "I guess I forgot that for a little while, but it's true. I won't do it again."

"You sure?" he asked finally.

"Yes," she said firmly. "I am very sure. It won't happen again."

Finally, he kissed her and finally, he relaxed against her, and finally, he wasn't mad anymore. He held her so tightly she could hardly breathe. But she didn't mind at all. She wished fervently that he was going to be at the cabin with her on practice day. But she had learned her lesson. Mentioning practice day to him meant mentioning cheerleading and, well, she was no fool. She kept her mouth shut and snuggled up against him.

The following day, Ardith Engborg decided

against lecturing them about the Garrison game. It could wait until they were at the lake cabin. At a brief meeting after school, she gave them last-minute instructions.

"I've been assured there is plenty of wood for the stove, so we won't freeze." She looked at Walt and Pres. "It'll be up to the two of you to get the fire going and keep it going. We've got plenty of food, so you'll all have a hot lunch."

She must have talked to my mother, Olivia thought dryly.

"Now," Ardith continued, "I can take some of you in my car. Who'll it be?"

"Olivia can ride with you," Walt said cruelly. "I'll take everybody else in my Jeep." After all, she hadn't wanted to sit with him on the bus.

Olivia's face turned scarlet.

"Hey, Walt, c'mon, . . ." Pres began, and Angie said quickly, "I'll ride with you, too, Mrs. Engborg."

Ignoring the look of misery on Olivia's face, Ardith said briskly, "Fine. Angie and Olivia with me. And I want all of you here, in the parking lot outside of school, at seven A.M. sharp. We'll divide up into two cars here."

She looked at each of them in turn and said, "Okay? Good, that's it, then. See you then!" and dismissed them.

Practice day was all set.

CHAPTER

Seven o'clock dawns very cold in the winter in the north country, but they were all there in front of the school when Ardith Engborg's blue sedan arrived.

"I smell snow," Ardith told Angie and Olivia as she led the way to the cabin on the lake, the Jeep following closely behind her.

"Well, it better not snow before we get back to town," Olivia joked, "or my mother will be out to get us in the town snowplow!"

"It's not supposed to," said Ardith. "I checked the forecast before I left the house. Of course, the forecast has been wrong more than once. We'll just have to keep an eye on that sky. If we see snowflakes, we'll head for home right away."

It took them more than half an hour to reach the cabin. Set deep in the woods, in a clearing facing the lake, the cabin was made of logs, built long and low with a front porch across its width.

"It's adorable!" Angie cried, getting out of the

car. "I love it! It's so romantic! It must be delicious in the summertime when the lake isn't frozen over."

"Well, I'll bet it's not romantic *inside*," Nancy said sourly. "I'll bet it's just plain frigid!" She was beginning to miss Josh already. He had crawled out of his nice warm bed this morning to drive her to school. She was sure it was his way of telling her that he did understand how important cheerleading was to her.

Well, it was. But she would rather be spending the whole day with Josh. She certainly hoped they got what they needed here at the lake, so it wouldn't be a total waste of time.

"Walt," Ardith ordered, "you and Pres grab some wood and go in and get a fire started in the stove. We'll unload the cars."

By the time they'd unloaded and taken their gear inside, the cabin had lost the frigid temperature Nancy had predicted, but it was still cold. They kept their jackets on while they checked out their surroundings.

The room they would be using was long and narrow, sparsely furnished. The pot-bellied stove Walt and Pres were tending was set back against the far wall, out of their way, and there was a huge picture window on the opposite wall, overlooking the lake.

"We'll heat our lunch on the stove," Ardith said. "There is a small bathroom by the back door. You can use that if necessary."

"Oh, good," Nancy said with relief. "I was afraid this place only had an outhouse."

Mary Ellen caught Pres's eye and grinned. "Is

she trying to pretend she actually knows what an outhouse is?"

He laughed. Nancy made a face, tossing her long brown hair. "I do. Lots of the lake cabins have them. I'm just glad this one doesn't."

"We know, Nancy," Mary Ellen said, moving closer to Pres, smiling up at him as if they shared a secret, "you're the kind of person who goes camping in a trailer complete with icemaker, color television, and a sauna."

Pres laughed again. Nancy's cheeks reddened. "What is this, Mary Ellen?" she asked sharply. "Am I your target for the day? Pick on somebody else!"

"Aw, poor Nancy!" Mary Ellen said, laughing as she turned away and sat down on the hardwood floor to trade her new boots for sneakers.

"All right, girls, that's enough!" Ardith ordered. She was not amused by Mary Ellen's teasing. "We came here to work, and I don't want any bickering."

She rubbed her hands together briskly. The stove was sending out welcome waves of warmth. It was time to get to work.

"Walt, did you remember to bring the portable tape player?"

He had, and while the others removed their jackets and did their stretching exercises, he put on a warm-up tape.

"All right, folks!" their coach said, clapping her hands together. "Let's put the last two games behind us and get to work!"

The warm-up exercises did exactly what Ardith Engborg intended them to do: It woke them all up. It sent the blood coursing through sluggish, sleepy, young bodies. She could almost pinpoint the exact moment when they became fully alert. A look passed among them that said, We're here!

She saw that look and thought, Good! Maybe out here in the middle of nowhere, without any distractions, you'll all start turning to each other again the way you used to. The way you're supposed to.

She certainly hoped so. As fond as she was of all of them, this lack of teamwork was beginning to fray her nerves. And heaven knows the last several games had been exercises in embarrassment, as much for her as for them. Would this day of concentrated practice do what she wanted it to?

By ten o'clock that morning, she was depressingly aware that the answer to that question was a resounding no. And she couldn't figure out why. Although it was cloudy and cold outside, it was cozy and warm in the cabin. They were all dressed properly, and they had the right music. And there were no distractions. But something was very wrong. She gave them a specific set of routines to follow and as they began, she sat on the floor, her tiny frame resting against one leg of the wooden table, and studied each cheerleader in turn.

Angie was fine, as always, a natural athlete whose graceful movements seemed totally effortless.

Nancy was executing her movements well enough, but it seemed to Ardith that she lacked enthusiasm.

"This is not a day of mourning," Ardith called out, "so could we show a little life here, please?"

Was it her imagination or were Pres and Mary Ellen flirting with each other every chance they got? Weren't they standing too close together when a routine didn't include them, and weren't they making an unusual amount of eye contact?

She didn't think it was her imagination. Mary Ellen looked prettier than ever in her pink leotard and black tights. Pres must have noticed, because he seemed to be having trouble keeping his eyes off her. And Mary Ellen knew he was watching her. While having an audience was usually just the thing to get Mary Ellen going, in this case it might be interfering with her concentration at the same time. *Something* certainly was, she thought grimly, as Mary Ellen wobbled on Walt's shoulders.

"Mary Ellen, pay attention! And Walt, try a smile! I promise you your face won't crack!"

Pres seemed as nervous as a caged tiger. Tension radiated from his body, making his movements sharp and jagged, like a marionette whose strings were too tight.

"Pres, for heaven's sake, loosen up!"

He flushed and glanced at Mary Ellen. She winked.

Oh, good grief! Ardith thought, extremely annoyed. So his nervousness is almost certainly sexual tension. She was aware of Pres's reputation. She also knew his steady girl friend, Kerry Elliot, was younger and seemed less sophisticated than Pres's other girls.

Girls like Mary Ellen Kirkwood.

Why doesn't he make the cheerleading work *for* him? Ardith wondered. If he would just relax and let his pent-up energy out in healthy, strenuous exercise, he'd feel one hundred percent better.

She switched her focus to Olivia, who hadn't been herself for some time now. Ardith shook her head as Olivia glanced Walt's way just as she began a cartwheel, and ended it by bumping into Nancy.

"Hey, for Pete's sake, watch what you're doing!"

Olivia reddened and mumbled an apology.

It was painfully obvious that Olivia and Walt hadn't made up. The usually graceful Walt was every bit as clumsy and uncoordinated as a rank beginner would have been. And Walt was no beginner.

I hate romances involving two squad members, Ardith thought vehemently. And if Mary Ellen doesn't ease up on Pres, I'm going to lock her in the bathroom because I simply can't take post-adolescent intrigue from more than one couple at a time! I can tell them how to make their bodies work well for them, she admitted ruefully as she got up to call a break, but I can't do a thing about their emotions.

She blew her whistle.

"Ten minute break," she said crisply. "You all seem to need it. Somebody help me put juice and fruit on the table."

While they were snacking, she went outside to check for signs of oncoming snow.

As Ardith left the cabin, Mary Ellen walked

over to Olivia, who stood alone at the picture window, looking out.

"So, how's Patrick these days?"

"Fine," Olivia answered casually, continuing to stare out the window.

"Funny," Mary Ellen pressed on, a slight edge to her voice, "I never thought you and Patrick would end up together."

Walt, standing at the table with the others, heard the name Patrick and looked up. With an orange slice halfway to his mouth, he stopped listening to what Nancy was saying and strained his ears instead for Olivia's answer.

"Oh, for heaven's sake, Mary Ellen," she said with a laugh, "Patrick and I are just friends."

"Right," Mary Ellen said coolly.

"Well, it's *true*," Olivia insisted, as Walt hung on every word. "Patrick's a nice person."

"I *know* that. I knew it before you ever even knew Patrick Henley was alive."

Walt absentmindedly put the orange slice in his hand back on the paper plate.

"Gross!" Angie cried. "Walt, you already handled that! You practically had it in your mouth. *I'm* not eating it."

Walt wasn't listening.

"Yes, I know you knew him first," Olivia replied, reaching down to adjust her red leotard. "But you didn't *want* him, remember?"

She walked away, leaving Mary Ellen standing by the window, her blue eyes narrowed in anger.

Walt kept hearing the words, "Patrick and I are just friends," over and over in his head. Did she really mean that? He had to find out. Maybe at lunch. . . .

"Pres!" Mary Ellen called in a bright voice, "Pres, c'mere a minute! Look at this stupid bird out on the lake. It's so dumb, it doesn't even know the lake is frozen. He'll probably die of thirst sitting out there and waiting like that."

Pres came over and stood beside her. He was very conscious of her nearness and as if she sensed that, Mary Ellen leaned against his arm and looked up at him, smiling, as she pointed at the bird.

Pres wasn't stupid. He knew an invitation when he saw one. And if no one else had been in the cabin, he knew that the moment wouldn't have passed without him kissing Mary Ellen. He wanted it, and so did she.

Maybe at lunch. . . .

Snow is definitely approaching, Ardith thought as she scanned a dark gray sky. But it might not start for hours. She would just have to keep checking. Ardith Engborg could think of a million things more fun than being stranded in a blizzard with six teenagers. Like cleaning the oven or getting rabies shots, she thought, grinning, as she went back into the cabin.

CHAPTER

The break hadn't helped. Ardith's slight frame marched back and forth in front of her squad as they performed after their snack, her short blonde hair bouncing angrily about her face as she tried to summon up some teamwork.

"Let's put some life in this! Pres, will you *please* relax! Mary Ellen, pay attention to the others. You're all supposed to be a team! Olivia, Walt, Nancy, could you please try a smile or two?"

But it was hopeless. Whatever was going on, it was affecting the whole squad, yet at the same time, separating them from each other.

Even Angie, while still responding well athletically, was losing her concentration. She, like Ardith, couldn't figure out why this day of practice wasn't working.

At twelve o'clock sharp, Ardith called a lunch break. Maybe some hot food would do what she hadn't been able to so far. But she wasn't terribly optimistic. Their morning snack certainly hadn't helped.

"Set up the food," she ordered wearily. "Pres and Walt, bring some more wood from the back porch. Then you can all relax for an hour." She looked straight at Pres as she stressed the word *relax*.

He shrugged.

"You may go outside after you eat if you want, but don't go far. I don't want to waste time organizing a search party."

Mary Ellen stopped Pres on his way to the woodpile. "Want to go exploring after lunch?" she asked softly, smiling up at him.

"Exploring *what*?" he asked suggestively, grinning.

She gave him a little punch in the chest. "The woods. Okay?"

He nodded. "Yeah, sure. Why not? I'm getting cabin fever in here."

"Meet you outside in fifteen minutes." Mary Ellen went to help the others put lunch on the table, ignoring Nancy's look of disgust.

Big deal. Why doesn't she just mind her own business, Mary Ellen thought resentfully. Pres is a big boy. He can take care of himself. Let her stick to her own boyfriend and quit worrying about Kerry's.

It occurred to Pres a few minutes later, as he pushed a small log into the stove, that he was playing with fire in more ways than one. He and Mary Ellen were a volatile combination.

But Kerry didn't trust him, anyway. And out here in the middle of nowhere, what difference did it make? If he didn't get out of this stupid cabin, he was going to explode!

Olivia ate her soup quickly, slipped into her jacket, and left the cabin. Her heart was pounding as she walked down to the lakefront, her hands in her jacket pockets. Would Walt follow her? He had to. He just *had* to.

"Hey, wait up!"

It was Walt. She turned to see him loping after her across the old snow and her heart jumped into her throat. He caught up with her. There was a long, awkward silence before he said, "Okay if I walk with you?"

Was he kidding? She smiled to show that it was indeed okay. The chance she'd been waiting for was finally here. They were going to be alone.

They crunched along the shore under a dark gray sky. "We're going to have a blizzard," Olivia said finally, unable to stand the silence another second. Besides, somebody had to say something. It might just as well be her.

"Yeah, sure looks like it. I hope we don't get stuck out here."

"Well, you don't have to worry. You've got the Jeep." Even though you wouldn't let me ride in it, was her unspoken accusation.

Walt knew it had to be talked about. He couldn't keep putting it off. They were moving too far away from the cabin, so he put a hand on her arm to stop her.

"I'm sorry about yesterday," he said slowly, looking down at her. "I was mad because you sat with Pres on the bus."

"That wasn't *my* idea!" Olivia protested. "I

think Pres thought he was doing me a favor. He thought you were going to snub me, and he didn't want me to be embarrassed."

"But I *was* going to sit with you," he said. "I'd been thinking about it all day."

Her cheeks reddened. "Well, Pres didn't know that. Neither did I. But I wanted to sit with you, too."

"You did?" He wanted very badly to wrap his arms around her.

She nodded. "I wanted to clear things up. We never really talked about your party. I wanted to make you understand what happened."

"Oh, that. Listen, I got a little blitzed myself the other night. Now that I know what that stuff can do . . . well, I guess I shouldn't have been so rough on you."

Her eyes widened. "You got drunk?" She giggled. "Boy, are you dumb!"

The giggle was music to his ears. "Yeah, I am. At least, I have been lately." His expression became very serious. "Boy," he said, reaching for her, "have I missed you!"

"Oh, Walt," she said, smiling up at him. "I've missed you, too."

He'd almost forgotten what that smile could do to him. Pulling her into his arms, he bent his head and kissed that sweet, warm mouth he'd missed so much. She was as eager as he was, and lifted her arms to encircle his neck. She felt so good to him. He couldn't believe he had gone without her for so long.

So why did the image of Olivia sitting on Boomer's lap, kissing him, flash through his mind so clearly and sharply that before he could stop himself, he had withdrawn his mouth from hers and pulled his head back.

She knew, of course. He could tell by the pain in her eyes that she knew exactly what had happened.

"Oh, Walt," she whispered. And then she turned and hurried away from him, walking quickly at first, then breaking into a run.

He hadn't meant it. He hadn't. He *did* understand what had happened at the party that night. So why had he just stuck a knife into Olivia's heart?

When she had stumbled up the cabin steps and disappeared inside, he followed slowly. Fighting the urge to just climb into the Jeep and drive away, he went back in and joined the others, avoiding Olivia's eyes.

When Mary Ellen and Pres and Walt and Olivia had left the cabin and Ardith had gone outside to check the sky again, Nancy tried to calculate how many hours it would be before she could be with Josh again. She had never missed him so much.

Joining Angie at a wooden bench beside the stove, she commented, "Boy, Mary Ellen never gives up, does she? She knows perfectly well that Pres is Kerry's private property. *Supposed* to be, anyway. And she still can't leave him alone! I'd kill her if she ever acted like that around Josh."

"I think she's lonely," Angie replied. "And I know what that feels like, so I guess I can't blame her too much."

Nancy looked at her in surprise. "You? Lonely?

I never think of you that way. You're so popular. You always seem to be in the middle of a crowd."

Angie's cheeks turned pink. "Well, I meant . . . not having someone special. I haven't been doing so well in the romance department since Marc found someone else. So I know how Mary Ellen feels."

Nancy sipped from her cup before replying. "Okay. But I don't see *you* making a play for someone else's boyfriend."

Angie laughed. "What on earth would Pres want from me? I'm not his type at all."

Nancy raised her eyebrows. "Are you kidding? The same thing he wants from Mary Ellen. Or any girl!"

Angie, always uncomfortable with gossip, changed the subject. She was perfectly content to eat the rest of her lunch listening to Nancy talk lovingly about Josh. It made her feel good. Boyfriend of her own or not, it was nice to know someone else had a healthy romance going.

Especially since the appearance a few minutes later of a tearful Olivia, followed by an obviously upset Walt, proved there had been no reconciliation there.

And heaven only knows, Angie thought as she finished the last of her soup, what Mary Ellen and Pres are up to.

What Mary Ellen and Pres were "up to" was wandering in the woods behind the cabin. They were holding hands as they stepped over fallen trees and mounds of old snow.

Mary Ellen glanced up at the darkening sky just as Olivia had, and said lightly, "Wouldn't it be funny if we got stranded out here?"

"Oh, hilarious," Pres said sarcastically, helping her over a tree stump. "I can't think of anything more fun than being stuck out here for the weekend!"

She stopped and smiled up at him. Tipping her head to look into his eyes, she said softly, "Would it really be so terrible? I can think of worse things."

Pres had known Mary Ellen for a long time, and he knew exactly what she was doing. He just hadn't made up his mind what to do about it.

Flirting with Mary Ellen was fun. Being with this beautiful girl got his juices flowing and made life more interesting. This whole stupid day would be boring him to death if it hadn't been for fun and games with her. There had to be more to life than just school, cheerleading, and dating only one girl, especially a girl who didn't trust him as far as she could throw him. And why should he behave himself when Kerry was so sure he *wasn't* behaving? What good would it do him to turn Mary Ellen down? Kerry wouldn't believe it, anyway.

"Depends," he answered Mary Ellen. "I guess that just depends on you."

And he pulled her to him and kissed her, just as they had both known he would all along.

Mary Ellen always felt terrific to Pres. Even outside on a cold, dark day in the middle of the woods, she felt good. He enjoyed kissing Mary Ellen as much as he'd ever enjoyed anything. Except kissing Kerry, of course. But Kerry wasn't *here*. And Mary Ellen was.

And glad to be, if he could judge by the way she was returning his kisses. He stopped kissing her just long enough to open his eyes and look down at her beautiful face, lifted toward him, her eyes closed.

Was anybody prettier than Mary Ellen?

"Hey," she murmured in protest without opening her eyes, and tightened her grip around his neck.

Even as he resumed kissing her, his eyes were casting about for a place where they could sit down. They couldn't stand here like this forever. He had just spotted what looked like the perfect place, a secluded area in a grove of small trees, when Ardith's whistle pierced the air. They both groaned. Breathing heavily, they separated and straightened their clothes and hair.

"Lousy timing," Pres grumbled.

"Right," Mary Ellen agreed. "I was just getting warmed up."

"So I noticed," he said, grinning.

She laughed. "Want to run away and hide for the rest of the afternoon? We could always say we got lost in the woods."

They both knew that was impossible.

He shook his head regretfully, and took her hand to lead her back to the cabin.

She began chattering almost immediately, which annoyed him. Did she have to take the interruption so lightly? Hadn't it meant anything to her? Of course it hadn't. He knew that. He'd known it the whole time. And if he was going to be really honest, it hadn't meant that much to him, either. He'd wanted it to, because it felt so good. But it hadn't.

She'd probably been pretending he was Patrick Henley. If he told her that, she would probably stare at him and say, "So? Weren't *you* thinking of Kerry?"

Well, yes, he had been. Some. But she could at least pretend to be a little upset about not being able to finish what they'd started. She ran up the steps ahead of him as if the cabin was exactly where she wanted to be.

All he wanted to do was go home.

CHAPTER

 16

As the afternoon session got underway, Ardith was forced to face the fact that the atmosphere in the cabin hadn't improved. The lunch break hadn't helped at all.

Olivia and Walt had obviously had another argument. There were faint streaks of smeared mascara on Olivia's cheeks, and Walt carefully avoided looking at her.

How can they work together if they won't even look at each other? Ardith thought, exasperated.

Although Pres and Mary Ellen had stopped flirting with each other, he was as tense as he had been earlier, and his movements were stilted and forced. He looked incredibly bored.

Nancy and Angie were trying, but Nancy was much too quiet and Angie was simply confused by everything that was going on around her.

It was impossible to expect anything positive to happen under such conditions. As far as

Ardith Engborg was concerned, this entire day had been a complete waste of time. Meanwhile, the sky outside grew blacker and blacker.

She finally threw in the towel. She blew her whistle. When she had their attention, she stood in front of them and announced that they were calling it quits.

She felt the enormous sigh of relief, although they hid it well. But she had no intention of letting them off the hook without a word.

"We are quitting partly because of the threat of bad weather," she said clearly, "but that is not the only reason. I am bitterly disappointed with each and every one of you."

Six people studied the hardwood floor.

"A lot of planning went into this day," she continued, "and I had high hopes for it. You all needed it desperately. I told you to bring the very best you had."

She paused to give her comments added weight.

"If what I've seen today is the very best you have," she said, "you have no business calling yourselves a cheerleading squad at all. I have never seen such a complete lack of teamwork in my life."

Mary Ellen raised her head long enough to direct a nasty glance toward Olivia and Walt.

Ardith saw the look and snapped, "I am speaking to *all* of you!"

Mary Ellen flushed and lowered her eyes.

"I don't want to talk about this any more right now," Ardith concluded. "But I would strongly advise all of you to go home and do some serious thinking about whether or not you have any interest in remaining Varsity Cheerleaders. Because if you do, you're going to have to prove it to me. Now get your things together and get this place cleaned up."

As they turned away, silent and subdued, she added, "Walt, you can take everyone home. Considering my present frame of mind, I seriously doubt that anyone would be comfortable riding in my car."

Walt nodded.

"That is," Ardith added in a voice filled with disgust, "if you can *stand* each other's company that long."

The cabin filled with an uncomfortable silence as Walt and Pres put out the stove fire and the others packed up everything and loaded the cars. When they had all piled into the Jeep, their coach warned Walt to go straight home.

"Don't make any side trips," she said when she had locked the cabin. "That sky looks very nasty. Could be just a squall, but it could also be a blizzard, so don't take any chances."

Satisfied that everything was in order, she went to her car and got in. Just as she pulled out of the clearing, followed by the Jeep, the first few snowflakes began drifting down.

The atmosphere inside the crowded Jeep was tense and silent. It was no comfort to any of them that the rest of the day was theirs. Ardith's words rang in their ears.

The Jeep was traveling far too sluggishly to suit Nancy. The blue sedan had already disappeared from sight, and the Jeep seemed to her to be practically standing still.

"Walt, can't you go any faster?" she complained, anxious to get back to Josh.

"You need new points and plugs," Pres called to Walt from the backseat where he was crammed between Olivia and Mary Ellen. "This thing runs like a dying cow."

The Jeep's engine sputtered, coughed, and died.

"You hurt its feelings, Pres," Angie joked. "It committed suicide."

"Walt?" Olivia asked timidly from her position beside Angie.

Walt stared out the windshield, quickly being covered with snow. "I can't believe I did this," he said quietly.

"What exactly is it that you did, Walt?" Mary Ellen asked, biting off her words one at a time. She was sick to death of this whole stupid day. All she wanted to do was get home. Why weren't they moving?

Five people looked at the Jeep's gas gauge as Walt silently pointed a gloved finger at it. The needle rested smugly at the very farthest point on the "Empty" side.

"You're not out of *gas*?" Nancy cried. "Oh, I don't believe this! Walt, you *knew* we were coming all the way out here today!"

Before they could all jump on Walt, Olivia said quietly, "It's okay. Walt always carries an extra can of gas in back, don't you, Walt?"

Walt groaned and leaned over the steering wheel, his head in his hands.

145

"Does that disgusting noise you just made mean what I think it does?" Mary Ellen asked, leaning over the back of the seat to look at Walt.

He nodded. "I brought all that gear with me," he explained, "— the tape player and the lanterns and the cooler for juice and stuff. I took the gas can out to make room for all of it."

Five people looked at him, knowing what was coming.

"I forgot to put it back in," he finished softly. "It's still sitting outside the garage door at my house."

No one said a word. They all sat there, staring out the windshield, now a solid barrier of white between them and the outside world.

Mary Ellen finally broke the silence. "I think," she said slowly, "that we had better get going if we don't want to be buried in this Jeep. Has everyone got boots and gloves?"

"Are you crazy?" Nancy cried, turning her head to stare at Mary Ellen. "We can't walk back to town in this snowstorm! We'd never make it. It's too far and it's too cold and it's snowing too hard."

"Do you have a better idea?"

"*I* do," Pres said. "It's simple. We just cut across the lake."

"You're even crazier than Mary Ellen," Nancy said coldly. "I'm not crossing that lake. I don't swim that well."

"Nancy, the lake is frozen. It's been frozen for months. You don't swim in a frozen lake."

146

"You do if the ice breaks," Mary Ellen pointed out softly. Raising her voice, she added, "Pres, we've been warned a thousand times against crossing the lake when it's frozen. You know that."

Pres sighed. "Look, guys," he said wearily, "I'm tired and I'm cold and I figure I don't stand a chance of walking all the way to town in this storm. I just want to get home and forget today ever happened. We can get across that lake in half an hour and that's exactly what I intend to do. Are you with me? Or would you rather stay here and become Tarenton High's first Varsity Snowmen?"

Mary Ellen said in a matter-of-fact voice, "He's right. I hate to admit it, but he is. I'm with him. I say we try the lake."

"But maybe Ardith will notice we're not behind her and come back for us," Nancy argued hopefully.

"Are you kidding?" This from Walt. "She can't see that we're not behind her. Visibility is practically zero."

"If we can't see out there, how can we make it across the lake?" Angie asked sensibly.

"Well," Walt said, "I have the lanterns. There are three of them, that's one for each pair of us. And we didn't use them at the cabin, so there's plenty of oil."

"And we'll just have to stay really close together," Olivia added. "I think we should do it. Even if Ardith does notice we're not behind her, she might just think we went a different way."

"Anyway," Mary Ellen said firmly, "we can't afford to sit here and wait for her. We'd better get going, like right this minute!"

No one argued with her. And when Walt climbed down out of the Jeep, the others followed. They waited in the swirling snow while Walt and Pres got the lanterns and lit them.

"Now," Mary Ellen said, taking a lantern from Pres and holding it up high, "the most important thing is to stay together. Everyone got that? We stay in pairs to share the lanterns, but we also stay together as a group. We link hands, and we don't let go for any reason, okay?"

They all nodded silently.

Walt and Pres each held a lighted lantern. "Who goes with me?" Pres asked.

"Olivia, you stay with Walt," Mary Ellen decided, "Angie, you come with me and Nancy, you're with Pres. He'll save you if you fall in."

"That's not funny!" Nancy cried sharply, and her voice shook just a bit.

The wind came up, sending snow flying into their eyes and mouths. Mary Ellen could barely see the others. Although she knew it couldn't have been much more than two o'clock in the afternoon, it was as dark as night. She tried to forget the countless times she and Gemma had been warned against trying to cross the frozen lake. "No matter how solid it looks," her parents had warned, "you just can't tell about ice."

Well, they had no choice. Trying to walk all the way back to town would be just plain stupid. It was the ice or nothing.

"Everybody hold hands," Mary Ellen repeated, "and *don't* let go!"

Single file, each of them clutching someone's hand, they crossed the highway and plodded down over the embankment to the lakeshore. Three lanterns held high provided necessary light and a warming glow that made the storm a little less frightening.

When they reached the shore, Mary Ellen suggested they test the ice along the edge by dropping a heavy rock on its surface.

"And just where are we going to find a rock in all this snow?" Pres asked sarcastically.

He had a point. They were standing in a sea of white.

"I don't know," Mary Ellen said helplessly, "but we really have to test the ice first. Especially along the shoreline, where it's the weakest."

"Right!" Pres agreed and, handing Nancy his lantern, he disappeared.

They heard thudding noises and then he was back, grinning as he emerged from the curtain of white that had hidden him.

"It's okay," he said, retrieving his lantern, "I promise. I jumped up and down on it. It's not even shaky."

"Well, *that* was bright," Mary Ellen snapped. "Supposed you'd fallen in. Then what?"

"Then you'd know the ice wasn't safe and you'd have to figure out something else."

He said this so matter-of-factly, and it was so true, that Mary Ellen had to laugh. "And you'd be drowned or frozen to death," she said. "Honestly, Pres, you're impossible!"

"This is true. Now let's cut out the chatter and get going."

"Thanks for trying the ice for us," Mary Ellen said, meaning it. They were all scared to death to set one foot onto that ice. Pres had made it just a little bit easier.

"Walt, you and Olivia go first," she said, anxious now to get going. "Pres and Nancy, you go next, and Angie and I will bring up the rear. We'll have to take turns holding up the lanterns. It's hard on the shoulder muscles. And whatever you do, do *not* let go of that hand you're holding!"

The only good thing about all of this, Nancy thought as she followed Pres gingerly onto the ice, wishing with all her heart that he was Josh, is that we're all dressed properly. The exercise gear under their jeans and jackets provided extra insulation, and they all had gloves, boots, and hats, except for Pres, who never wore anything on his head. His dark blond hair was a thatch of powdery white.

The ice felt as solid as ground under their feet, as they began their trek, single-file, hands linked, across the frozen lake.

Within minutes, Pres's eyes were watering, his ears felt as if they were encased in ice, and his shoulders ached from holding the lantern high. But he felt . . . useful, for the first time in a long time. He liked the feeling.

Although they were all anxious to reach safety on the opposite shore, it was slow going. They were fighting wind and snow all the way. Their faces and clothes were stiff with cold and wet snow. The ice felt solid enough, but still they inched along cautiously.

Mary Ellen kept hearing her father's voice: "You never can tell about ice."

Ardith Engborg had been driving for about fifteen minutes when it suddenly struck her that there was no Jeep behind her. Even in the storm, she should have been able to see at least a faint glow from Walt's lights. But there was nothing.

She slowed down. She hated to pull off the road and risk getting stuck on the shoulder, but she couldn't keep going until she was sure her squad was somewhere behind her. This day at the lake had been her idea. She was responsible for them.

Where on earth were they?

She gave it another five minutes before seeking out a place to turn the car around. A driveway finally appeared, and in minutes she was retracing the path she'd just driven. The strong sense of relief that flooded her when her headlights made out the Jeep, left her the moment she realized it was empty.

Parking the sedan, she got out, her coat whipping around her in the wind. Ardith Engborg was not a woman who frightened easily, but standing beside the empty Jeep, she was conscious of hands that shook and a stomach with a sudden hole in it.

Where *were* they?

Pulling herself together, she checked the back of the Jeep and found the lanterns missing. So wherever they'd disappeared to, they at least

151

had light. Had they gone back to the cabin? It was locked, but they could figure out a way to get in. If she went to the cabin, would they be there?

Ardith couldn't have said what made her turn and look out over the lake. She stared across it. *No*. They wouldn't have. They all knew better.

So that couldn't be the faint glow of lanterns, that dull bit of dim light out there on the lake. It was so faint she would have dismissed it, except for one thing. There shouldn't have been *any* light at all out on the lake. None. No one would be ice fishing in this weather.

Dear God, she thought with sickening certainty, they're out there on that ice! She ran for her car, slipping in the snow, her heart thudding in her chest.

What Ardith was unable to see from where she'd been standing was that her Varsity Cheerleaders were at that moment about to leave the ice.

Walt, leading the frozen, weary parade had just set foot on shore. "We made it!" he shouted over his shoulder, hoisting his lantern high so they could all see how close they were to safety.

Five people broke rank, shouting, "Halleluia!" and made a run for the shore.

There was a sudden, sickening crack and Mary Ellen watched in horror and disbelief as Angie Poletti, whose hand she had been holding only a split second earlier, disappeared into a yawning black hole in the ice.

CHAPTER

There was that one horrible split second that would haunt them for a long time to come, when they were all seized with the urge to flee, to race off the ice to safety, escaping a fate identical to Angie's now struggling in the black, icy water.

Mary Ellen saw it in their faces and understood it. She felt it, too.

But fighting and defeating that urge, she snapped into action.

"Let's go!" she shouted at the others who stood, frozen in shock along the shoreline. "We've got to get her out of there!"

Instantly, they came as close as they dared and waited for more commands from Mary Ellen.

"Angie, stop thrashing around!" was her second command. She knew Angie's natural instincts as an athlete were sending her a dangerous message — that she could save herself. She couldn't. Not only was she weighted down with a ton of sodden, heavy winter clothing, but Mary

153

Ellen was sure the icy water would numb her body in minutes, if not seconds.

"Stay still, Angie," she ordered. "You're just making things worse. We'll get you out."

Setting her lantern off to one side, she called to the others, "Human chain! Hurry! Everyone lie flat on the ice. Walt, you be the anchor on shore. Nancy, Walt will get a good grip on your ankles, and you do the same with Olivia. Pres, you get behind me. Hurry!"

Although Mary Ellen sounded perfectly in control of the situation as everyone scrambled to obey her orders, she was terrified. The ice surrounding the hole looked like the wire spokes on the wheels of Pres's Porsche: jagged lines radiating out on all sides from where Angie's head bobbed. The rest of the ice could go at any second, and Mary Ellen knew it.

At least, she thought gratefully as she knelt carefully, then lay flat on her stomach with Pres holding her ankles, it's stopped snowing so hard. I can *see* Angie.

It was not a pleasant sight. Angie had obeyed Mary Ellen's orders and stopped flailing about. She was barely managing to keep her arms above her head, her hands clinging to the broken edges of the ice to keep her head above water. But her lips were blue, her face waxy-white, her hair under the knitted cap clinging to her cheeks and coated with tiny droplets of ice. Her teeth were chattering with such force that Mary Ellen was afraid she would bite off her tongue.

Everyone held their breath as Mary Ellen unclasped first Angie's left hand, then her right, and held them tightly in her own hands.

Sure that she had a firm grip, she twisted her head to call, "Okay, everybody, *pull*. Pull hard!"

Walt, lying flat on the shore, inched his body backward, pulling Nancy with him.

Everybody moved except Mary Ellen and Angie.

"Pull harder!" Mary Ellen shouted. "I can't *lift* her!"

They pulled again. Nothing.

"Let me switch places with you," Pres said. "Maybe I can lift her out."

Mary Ellen shook her head. "No, the ice won't support that much movement. It probably wouldn't even support you up here. It's too weak around the edges. Stay where you are."

Once more, she shouted, "Pull!" and again nothing happened, except that her ankles burned where Pres was pulling on them.

She rested her head on her arm. We can't do this, she thought with a certainty that hit her in the chest like a hammer. We can't. We're not going to get her out of there. The thought was so repugnant that it propelled her head up off her arm and gave her back her voice.

"Angie," she pleaded, "you've got to help us. We can't do this by ourselves, okay? Try to pull yourself up. Pretend you're chinning yourself on the ice. Then you can make your hands climb up my arms, just as if you were climbing the rope in gym class, okay?"

Angie's clear blue eyes, looking up into Mary Ellen's face, remained blank.

"Angie, please," Mary Ellen begged, trying

not to cry, "please try. We all have to work together on this one, just like we always do, all right?"

Angie stared dully at her captain.

Mary Ellen felt tears on her cheeks. "Angie," she said sternly, "you can't stay in there forever. We have a game Tuesday night, remember?"

Nothing.

In desperation, Mary Ellen turned her head to cry out, "For God's sake, I need *help* here! She's not hearing me!"

From somewhere behind her came a weak, "Go, Angie!" Then another, a bit louder. Maybe from Nancy. Mary Ellen couldn't tell whose voice it was. Then she heard Walt's voice from shore calling, "Go, Angie!" and that was followed by Olivia and Nancy calling in one voice, "Go, Angie!"

And then a chorus, one louder, stronger voice from all of them together: "Go, Angie, go, Angie, go, Angie!" came in cadence, echoing across the ice repeatedly, shouted with increasing determination.

A flicker of recognition appeared in Angie's eyes.

"It's working!" Mary Ellen shouted. "Keep it up!"

Her squad obeyed and the ice reverberated with sound.

To Angie, she said, "Hear that? It's just like at a basketball game. Only *we're* playing this time. And you've got a jump shot, Angie. All you have to do it stretch up and go for it."

"Go, Angie, go, Angie, go, Angie!" from behind them.

Angie looked up at Mary Ellen and tried to raise her body in the water. The ice made ominous creaking sounds.

"Get this jump shot, Angie," Mary Ellen urged. "C'mon, you can do it!"

Angie tried again, and failed, and this time her body sank lower in the water and her arms pulled at Mary Ellen's grip.

"Oh, dammit, Angie," Mary Ellen sobbed, "you get up here and get that jump shot or you're off this squad right now, you *hear* me?"

"Go, Angie, go, Angie, *go*, Angie!"

Slowly, very slowly, Angie forced her heavy, water-laden body upward. The strain of the effort showed in her waxen face, and Mary Ellen, wanting so desperately to help, stretched her own body forward as far as she dared to make it easier on her teammate.

It seemed to a sobbing Mary Ellen to take forever but Angie's hands climbed slowly, slowly up her captain's arms until Mary Ellen was able to clutch the frozen girl around her upper chest.

"Pull!" she screamed to the others. "Slide backward and pull as hard as you can!"

To Angie, she gasped, "Now, Angie, just put your arms around my neck. You'll be out of there in a second."

As Angie reached up to obey Mary Ellen's instructions once more, icy water cascaded from her, pouring over Mary Ellen's hands and arms, already frozen with cold.

But she couldn't quit now.

The others weren't quitting, either. Now that Mary Ellen and Angie had done their part, the rest of the line stopped chanting in order to save their breath and energy, and began sliding backward and pulling with renewed vigor.

It was slow, painful work, done by bodies chilled to the bone and already exhausted. But they didn't stop. It wasn't until Angie was completely free of the last trace of cracking ice that Mary Ellen shouted, "Okay, we're clear!"

Then they all collapsed onto the ice, breathing heavily, unable to believe it was over.

When Nancy sat up a minute or two later, she burst into tears, and Olivia did the same, but even as she started crying she crawled across the ice to Nancy and put her arms around her. "It's okay," she said through her tears. "It's okay. It's all over."

Pres wrapped his arms around a sodden Angie on one side and Mary Ellen on the other and said weakly, "Hey, guys, if it's all over, how come you're crying now?" and Olivia and Nancy laughed before they began crying again. Walt crawled over to the two girls and put an arm around each of them. "It's okay, it's okay," was all he could think of to say.

Mary Ellen gathered her strength together and stood up. With Pres's help, she pulled a water-laden and very shaky Angie to her feet.

Angie looked around at all of them as they got to their feet. "You all look absolutely terrible!" she said through chattering teeth, and managed a weak grin.

Nancy and Olivia stopped crying, and Walt announced in a husky voice, "If anything deserves a cheer, that smile does!"

Angie got a rousing "Angie — Angie — Rah! Rah! Rah!"

The realization of what had almost happened hit them all at the same time. The cheering stopped, the smiles left their faces, and they stared at Angie. She was soaking wet, very shaky and pale, and she looked like a rag doll that had been tossed into a washing machine.

But she was alive.

That hole in the ice had been very dark. Angie could have disappeared into it and slipped out of their reach, making rescue impossible.

It could have happened just that way. They could have lost her. So quickly. . . .

Five people shuddered.

Walt's gaze went from Angie to Olivia. Her eyes were on his and they were dark with terror. She'd been thinking the same thing he had.

In a second, he turned her toward him and she was in his arms. He held her so tightly, she gasped. He couldn't stop thinking that it could just as easily have been Olivia in that water. And she wasn't as strong as Angie was.

"Oh, Lord," he moaned into her hair, and she clutched him tightly. They stood there, clinging together as close as they could get, saying nothing.

Watching them, a shaken Pres cursed himself for being a fool. First with Vanessa, then with Mary Ellen that very afternoon (it seemed like years ago now). He had come as close to throwing away what he and Kerry had, as they had come to losing Angie. He didn't deserve Kerry. But it was Kerry he wanted. He was more sure of that than he'd ever been of anything.

Supporting a shaking Angie, fully aware of how lucky they were that she was standing there, he took a deep breath and let it out. Over Angie's head, his eyes met Mary Ellen's.

It's like this, was the message he sent her: I just found out that life is too short to spend it fooling around.

Mary Ellen gave him a shaky smile. Then she said softly, "Pres, thanks for doing such a good job of keeping me out of that water. I mean that!"

"You're *all* wonderful!" Angie said. "Every single one of you!"

Nancy stood off to one side, tears streaming down her face. She was wishing that Josh would suddenly appear at the top of the hill and come running down to wrap his arms around her.

"Yes, we *are* wonderful," Mary Ellen said, wiping her face with the sleeve of her jacket. She looked around at her teammates and announced clearly, "We *are*! Did we or did we not work with precision, cooperation, and utter, total concentration? Did we or did we not perform a mind-boggling display of exquisite teamwork? Did we or did we not," her voice gathering volume, "work together as one unit to save this precious girl's life?" She was grinning, her blue eyes shining.

"Hear, hear!" Walt shouted, lifting his head away from Olivia, but keeping his arms around her.

"Well," Pres said, grinning at Walt, "I always

said this girl would do anything for the squad, didn't I? Let's face it, her dip in the lake gave us back our old teamwork." Looking down at Angie, he added, "Don't you think that was just a little bit drastic, sweetheart?"

Angie smiled weakly. "The teamwork was never gone, Pres. It was just . . . misplaced." She looked around at the five of them, tears in her eyes. "I thank you," she said simply. "If you hadn't pulled together as a team, I —"

"Hey!" Mary Ellen interrupted, suddenly anxious for things to get back to normal, "why are we standing here talking about how wonderful we are when this poor girl is freezing to death? Now that we have our perfect teamwork back, we can't afford to lose one of us to pneumonia."

Nancy said, "I agree. Let's get off this stupid lake and go home." She glanced toward the top of the hill as if she still expected Josh to suddenly appear.

It wasn't Josh who appeared at the top of the hill. It was Patrick.

Out on his Saturday rounds when the storm hit, he had been passing the lake when he heard shouting. When he parked, got out, and looked down to see lights that shouldn't have been there, and saw the pathetic, bedraggled little group, he knew what had happened.

They watched him run down the hill and over to Mary Ellen's side. One look at Angie told him the whole story. Scooping her up in his arms, he said crisply, "We've got to get this girl into dry clothes. Like right *now*! C'mon, let's go!"

Happy to have someone else take over, Mary

Ellen followed him. The others were right behind her.

Ardith Engborg's blue sedan came to a sliding halt on the highway just as Patrick appeared, carrying Angie and flanked by the other cheerleaders.

Ardith caught her breath. Something terrible had happened.

"What happened here?" she asked sharply, as she reached the group gathered around Patrick's garbage truck.

Mary Ellen spoke up quickly. She explained clearly and honestly what had taken place.

"We're sorry," she finished. "We are very, very sorry. We thought it was the safest thing to do at the time. If we'd known the storm was just a squall, we'd have waited in the Jeep or gone back to the cabin. But we were afraid we'd be stranded. Anyway," she finished, "I think you would have been proud of us. We all worked together to get her out. And we *did* it!"

She looked around at the others. "Didn't we?"

Olivia and Walt, their arms around each other, said proudly, "We sure did!"

"Teamwork all the way!" Pres agreed. "We hadn't lost it, after all. We'd just temporarily misplaced it."

"And finding it again means a lot to all of us, Mrs. Engborg," Nancy added quietly, "even though this was a terrible way to get it back."

"Are you all right?" Ardith asked Angie. "That's all I'm interested in right now."

Angie nodded. "I'm fine. At least I will be when I'm dried off." Then she added, "And what they told you is the truth. It was teamwork that saved my life. They just wouldn't give up, not a single one of them."

"I'm glad to hear that," Ardith said quietly, visibly shaken. "But you've got to get home and get dry clothes on before you freeze solid."

"Oh, I can't go home like this!" Angie cried. "If my mom saw me now, she'd have a coronary!"

"No problem," Patrick said heartily. "We'll just go to Mary Ellen's house. Right, Melon? You can lend Angie some dry clothes and get her cleaned up."

Under the circumstances, it no longer seemed important to Mary Ellen that none of the squad see the way she lived, in the modest little turquoise house.

"Sure," she said after only a moment's hesitation. "Let's go!"

Ardith offered to take the others home and then take Walt and his missing gas can back to the Jeep. Mary Ellen, watching them all climb into the sedan, felt a rush of warmth for her teammates. What would she have done if any one of them had decided to quit out there on the lake?

"See you!" she called, waving as they pulled away. Then she climbed into Patrick's truck to sit beside Angie.

CHAPTER

18

Watching Patrick gently tuck the edges of an old wool blanket under Angie's chin, Mary Ellen thought, Thank you, Patrick. Thank you for coming along when you did. Thank you for being so gentle with Angie. Thank you for . . . being Patrick.

He carried Angie into Mary Ellen's house and upstairs to the bathroom, following Mary Ellen's directions.

"A hot tub, right now!" she ordered Angie, showing her where everything was. "Soak until every inch of you feels warm. I'm going to fix you some hot tea. I'll be right back."

In the kitchen, she asked Patrick if he thought Angie should see a doctor. She put the teakettle on and got out the cups and teabags.

"She seems okay," he said. "Wait and see how she feels after the tub and the tea." He smiled. "If that works, you could always market it: Mary Ellen's Tub and Tea Cure. You'll become rich and famous." His smile disappeared. "And that's what you've always wanted, right?"

She sighed. Patrick looked so handsome standing there, leaning against the kitchen counter in his blue sweater and navy down jacket. And she was so grateful to him for helping out.

She moved closer to him, laying her head on his chest and putting her arms around his waist.

"You must think I'm such a snob," she said softly.

"No," he answered firmly, lifting her chin with his hand so he could look into her eyes. "I don't think you're a snob. But you see things differently than other people do. Like this kitchen, for example, this house. . . ."

"What about them?" She stood up straight, away from Patrick's chest, and looked around. The old yellow refrigerator, its door patterned with messages held on by strawberry magnets from the dime store; the old round dinette set, its fake-leather seats worn with age; the apple tree wallpaper that her mother had hung upside-down, all of it so familiar to her. That paper had hung unnoticed for months until one day Gemma had said, "Mom, why are the roots of the apple trees at the top instead of the bottom?"

They'd all had a good laugh over that wallpaper.

"This is a nice room, Mary Ellen," Patrick said, "and it's a nice house. Warm and friendly. You can stop worrying about what Angie will think of it, because I know she'll love it."

Mary Ellen's cheeks burned. She moved away to stand in front of the stove, holding her still-frozen hands above the heat coming from the steaming teakettle.

Suddenly he was behind her, his arms around her waist.

"And you look awfully good in this kitchen," he whispered in her ear.

She whirled and buried her face in his chest. She had been chilled to the bone and as he gathered her close, she felt warm and safe and excited. As she always did in Patrick's arms.

She raised her head and Patrick bent his. The kiss was a long, slow one, shaking both of them to their toes. Behind them on the stove, the kettle let out a shrill whistle.

"You can say that again!" Patrick said shakily, and Mary Ellen giggled.

Then his expression grew serious and as Mary Ellen lifted her head for another kiss, he shook his, saying, "Uh-uh. This is not a good idea."

Surprised, she stared up at him. "What's wrong?"

"What's wrong is, you've had one hell of a day, you're grateful that I showed up at the lake, and you don't know what you're doing. Tomorrow you'll be sorry. You always are."

"No, Patrick," she protested, but he removed her arms from around his waist, and walked away from her.

When he reached the door, he gave her a long look and said, "Believe me, Mary Ellen, what I want from you is a lot more than gratitude. When you can handle that, if you ever can, give me a call."

And he was gone, letting in a cold blast of air

as he opened the kitchen door and closed it after him. Mary Ellen was cold again. But she wasn't sure if it was from the blast of air, or because Patrick was no longer holding her. Maybe it was a little of both.

She went to the refrigerator to get milk for the tea and spotted a note from her mother under one of the strawberry magnets.

"M.E.," it read, "owner of Marnie's called. Fired Vanessa. Wants to know can you work two afternoons a week. Call her. Mom."

If Mary Ellen hadn't been so sore and stiff from her ordeal at the lake, she would have done half a dozen Flying Eagles right there in the kitchen. She had a job! Even two afternoons a week was better than nothing. And she'd be getting modeling experience. She couldn't believe it. She would call Mrs. Gunderson just as soon as she'd changed into the warmest bathrobe she owned and made sure Angie was okay.

She ran a hand gently over her mouth and smiled. She could still feel Patrick's kiss. And it felt wonderful.

Angie was fine. The hot tub, she said, had done a lot to warm her bones. Mary Ellen borrowed a fluffy pile robe from her mother's closet to wrap Angie in, and put on a robe of her own. Then they went downstairs to drink their tea.

When Mary Ellen had put a roast in the oven for dinner, she and Angie sat at the table, drinking hot tea and snacking on crackers. Heat from the oven warmed the small room, and the kitchen seemed cozy and comfortable. Mary Ellen could almost see Angie thawing as they talked about the afternoon, and she seemed very much at home, just as Patrick had said she would be.

Suddenly Angie giggled. Mary Ellen looked at her in surprise. "What?"

Angie shook her head, biting her lip to hold back laughter. "I was just remembering the very last thing you said to me when I was still in the water. It was just about the time that I realized I might not ever get out."

Mary Ellen looked blank. "What was it?"

Angie was trying valiantly to keep a straight face. "You said," she said, "that if I didn't do as I was told right that very minute, I was off the team!"

Mary Ellen frowned. "So?"

Angie's cheeks turned pink with repressed laughter. "Mary Ellen, I was *drowning*! At least, I thought I was. And there you were, threatening me!" She looked at Mary Ellen across the table, her blue eyes sparkling, her lips twitching at the corners.

Mary Ellen stared back at her. Then her lips, too, curved in a smile that quickly became a full-blown grin. "Well," she said, "it worked, didn't it?"

Angie's laughter exploded. She threw her head back and let peal after peal of delicious, tension-relieving laughter fill the kitchen.

It was contagious and Mary Ellen, realizing the absurdity of her last remark to Angie when she was in the water, no matter how effective it had been, let her own sense of humor take over. All of the tension of the past weeks, all of the horror of that afternoon, was washed away in wave after wave of unbridled hilarity.

When their stomachs began to ache from spasm after spasm of laughter, they lay back against their chairs, gasping for breath, tears streaming down their cheeks.

Mary Ellen gasped, "You realize this is sheer hysteria, don't you?"

Angie nodded wildly. "And I ask you," she said in a choked voice, "who has a better right?" Then she sobered up long enough to ask, "All I want to know is, would you *really* have kicked me off the squad if I'd drowned?"

"Well, of course," Mary Ellen said just as soberly, "because you wouldn't have shown up for practice, and that's an automatic dismissal." Then she gave in, shouting wildly, "Oh, God, that's so morbid! We must have the most perverted senses of humor in the world!" and they were both off again in wild gales of laughter until the phone rang, jarring them into sobriety.

Grabbing a box of tissues from the counter and handing it to Angie, Mary Ellen grabbed a handful and wiped her face. She took a deep, composing breath and answered the telephone.

It was Olivia. She and Walt wanted to know if Angie was okay and if there was anything they needed.

Mary Ellen had no sooner assured them that Angie was just fine and hung up, when the phone rang again. This time it was Nancy. Did they need anything at all at Mary Ellen's house, she wanted to know, because if they did, she and Josh would bring it right over. Cough medicine? Nose drops? Decongestants?

"She sounds like Olivia's mother," Mary Ellen whispered to Angie. Then she thanked Nancy and said no, they were just fine and didn't need a thing.

Ardith called, and Mary Ellen eased her mind about Angie and then told her Angie was staying the night, glancing quickly at Angie to see if that was okay with her. Angie nodded happily, adding that she would have to call her mother to get permission.

She had just hung up with permission granted, when Pres called. He was at Kerry's, but he could run right over there if Mary Ellen and Angie needed anything, anything at all.

"You see?" she asked Angie when she had hung up and resumed her seat at the table. "You see how nice it is being part of a team? All of those people really care about you."

"We all care about each other," Angie said quietly, smiling. "I know we forget that sometimes, but it's true. It the best part of being on the squad."

"No, it's not," Mary Ellen said soberly.

Angie looked at her, surprised. "It's not?"

"Of course not." Mary Ellen toyed with the handle of her cup. Then she looked straight at Angie and grinned. "The best part is wearing those cute little short skirts."

And they were once again convulsed with giggling that wouldn't quit.

What is making Olivia feel so strange? Read Cheerleaders #8, PLAYING GAMES.

Join the Team!

They're talented. They're fabulous-looking. They're winners! And they've got what you want! **Don't miss any of these exciting CHEERLEADERS books!**

Watch for these titles! $2.25 each